SUBSURDITY

SubSurdity

Vignettes from Jasper Lane

Eric Arvin

iUniverse, Inc.
New York Lincoln Shanghai

SubSurdity
Vignettes from Jasper Lane

iUniverse books may be ordered through booksellers or by contacting:

iUniverse
2021 Pine Lake Road, Suite 100
Lincoln, NE 68512
www.iuniverse.com
1-800-Authors (1-800-288-4677)

Because of the dynamic nature of the Internet, any Web addresses or links contained in this book may have changed since publication and may no longer be valid.

This is a work of fiction. All of the characters, names, incidents, organizations, and dialogue in this novel are either the products of the author's imagination or are used fictitiously.

ISBN: 978-0-595-45482-2 (pbk)
ISBN: 978-0-595-89794-0 (ebk)

Printed in the United States of America

To my mother and my aunts, Sandra & Joyce

This book was made possible through the unending support of those who responded so well to my first book, and the dilligence of my editor N.C. Strickland. Also, I owe a big "thanks" to my friend HvH (http://hvhexpo.blogspot.com/) for his gorgeous cover art.

CHAPTER 1

Melinda Louise Gold stood upright and proud on the side of the driveway, peering out over the perfectly manicured lawn. Not one blade of grass was longer than another, not a sneaky dandelion was in sight. In front of her she saw order and structure.

"Perfect," she sighed with a smile.

She had to admit, Frank could cut a good lawn. There wasn't much else to be said for him, but she hadn't married him for his personal qualities, had she? That was more to do with Nanna than anything, and—

Mustn't dwell on that, she chided herself.

His lawn-cutting abilities were admired by all the neighbors. He was meticulous, cutting in perfect lines, and trimming the rose bushes just so, the hedges clean. Unfortunately, Frank hadn't passed on the trait to their son Patrick. As a result, Melinda absolutely never allowed Patrick to get on the mower. The last time she had asked him to mow the lawn, it was cut so close that it was balded in spots. Her eyes still filled with tears of rage when she thought about it.

But that would not happen again. No sir-ee Bob! The only thing that concerned her about the lawn now was how to keep Ruth Goins' dog from relieving himself on the perfect grass. She discussed this with Ruth—the old woman hadn't even had the decency to put in her teeth as they spoke—but Ruth said that Gayhound had taken a liking to Melinda's lawn. She'd made it clear to Melinda that she would be darned if she would keep him from his bliss.

His bliss? Why, the very idea of dogs feeling bliss! They peed on fire hydrants and licked themselves. And what was with that name? Gayhound? As if an animal could be gay. Preposterous! Gay penguins and dogs, it was all an agenda. Her own mother had assured her of this, and she would know. Nanna was a member of Focus on the Family, after all.

Thankfully, the country was being led by a righteous man now. He was good with God, possibly even chosen. Melinda had to admit that it *was* strange he had been struck by a bolt of lightning in the White House Rose Garden. And it was stranger still that it happened on live TV as he was giving a national address on the evils of gay marriage. But add to all that the fact that it happened on a seemingly sunny day, and Melinda was convinced that it was surely a sign. The president had survived. She had convinced herself, as had Nanna, that the bolt was nothing more than God's index finger giving an overzealous love tap.

She fussed at her shiny blonde hair (that was not mussed) and straightened out the wrinkles from her elegant grey pant suit (that was not wrinkled), satisfied once again by the perfect facade her house presented to the neighborhood. "Look at me!" it shouted every morning.

As she turned to go back into the coolness of her air-conditioned, two-story house with wrap-around porch and a patio out back, she caught a glimpse again of the new arrival on Jasper Lane. Her hand involuntarily went to her chest as if she might calm her heart by the touch.

She had heard from Cassie Bloom that his name was James ... James Something-or-other. Melinda welcomed new neighbors. Why shouldn't she? One shouldn't judge people before meeting them. She knew that; the Bible told her so. But this man, this James, he ran around Jasper Lane half-naked, with no shirt and only a small pair of green shorts! It hardly hid his ... male parts!

He was a big man, too. Strong, with large muscles that twitched and flexed as he ran. Why, it was repulsive! Immoral even! A man of such an age—surely in his late twenties—running about in the middle of the day with his chest bouncing and his nip-. Melinda couldn't even think *that* word! *Nipples.* She gasped in the realization that she had even thought the word. She had even spelled it in her mind, letter by letter, as she watched the young man approaching with bouncing, sweaty ...

No! Melinda, stop!

What should she do? She couldn't turn and walk away. Surely he had seen her by now. No. She would make her stand and let her feelings be known. It was her neighborhood as well. In fact, it was more hers than his. She had lived in the same house for ten years, for mercy's sake!

She would put her foot down and tell him to jog wearing something more decent. Maybe he could wear a sweat shirt or a baggy t-shirt that wouldn't show off his … nipples.

Oh, that word!

As he approached, Melinda smiled pleasantly to show him she was only ever concerned with the welfare of those around her. There were children on this street. Weren't there? She was sure there were children somewhere. She raised her hand slightly, fingers wiggling with red nails.

"Mrs. Gold," the young man nodded between heavy breaths. He passed her by quickly and without incident, his feet striking the pavement hard and determined.

"Wait," she spoke, too low and too late. Her smile faded to a defeated frown.

Next time. Definitely tomorrow, she said to herself as she watched the muscular man's sweaty back and shoulders push through the humid air. Her hand returned to her chest. She suddenly felt very strange, almost faint. Her heart beat as if it would burst from her rib cage and follow young James Something-or-other of its own accord.

"My heavens!" she declared quietly, trying to banish that nuisance of feeling from her core.

As she watched James run farther down the street to the corner of the tree-lined avenue, a small, ugly blue vehicle rounded the turn. It swerved to the other side of the road as if James were an elephant and the driver was making gosh-golly-darned sure he was going to miss. The car ran up onto a curb and knocked over an empty trash can before correcting and getting back on course. Clearly, the driver was committing the sin of lust.

Melinda shook off her … whatever it was, and walked back into the house, self-consciously glancing from side-to-side. Her painted nails played at the top buttons of her pant-suit jacket. Cassie was coming for coffee. She should start getting things ready.

Rick Cooper pulled into the driveway, his heart still pounding from his run-in with the curb. More truthfully, it was the sight of a sweaty, beefy muscle god in tiny, green shorts that flustered him. He was still a tad dumbfounded by the experience. If things had gone worse, if he had run into a house instead of trash cans, there would have been serious repercussions. He only had one eye. It would be a clear-cut case to any police officer.

"Ricky, baby!" came a shout from the lawn. Terrence sat in his green lawn chair in the center of the grass, holding a very large margarita in one hand and a very small pink cell phone in the other. "I'll call you back," he said quickly to the person on the other end.

"Hey, Terrence," Rick greeted, as he got out of the rusty blue Festiva.

"Is this all you brought?" Terrence asked, somewhat disappointedly as he approached the vehicle, peering in the back seat. He held his drink like a prized possession, high and out of harm's way, sunglasses he had perched on his shaved head.

"I didn't have much," Rick answered, numbly. "Most of the stuff was Coby's."

"So, he gets everything? The apartment, the dog, the computer? The greedy slut!"

"Yeah, I didn't buy too much when we were together." Rick's reply was simple, nonconfrontational.

"Well, how could you? I mean, he was using everything you made to support his gambling habit," Terrence explained. "What an ass! And after your accident, too." He shook his head in disdain before taking a gulp from his glass as one hand stayed permanently fixed to his hip.

"Well, it's over now. All I've got are these few boxes of clothes and CDs."

"We'll soon fix that, baby!" Terrence grinned. "There are some fabulous places around here to shop."

Rick could always count on Terrence to know the best shopping venues. Even in college he could smell out a unique shopping experience a mile away. But then, unique never much appealed to Rick.

"I like the shaved look," Rick said, gesturing to Terrence's dome.

"Why, thank you, darlin'," Terrence replied in a faux southern accent. "I like the eye patch. It looks good on you. You can really pull that off."

"Whatever," Rick shrugged.

"No, really. Gives you character. It's sexy."

"I lost my eye, Terrence," Rick said. "That's not sexy."

"You didn't lose it. It was taken from you by that bastard of a boyfriend and his gambling debts. And then," he exclaimed, clearly getting more intoxicated by the minute, "he goes and breaks your glass eye! Who breaks someone's glass eye! I mean, really! You were living in a damn Tarantino film, my friend."

Rick laughed dryly. "It's good to see you, Terrence," he said, giving his friend a hug. "Thanks for this, for letting me move in. You and David are great friends."

"Don't mention it, hon. It's David's house, though. I'm just staying here for a bit, too. Want a margarita before we unpack you?" David and Terrence had been the best of friends since college, yet they couldn't have been more differ-ent. David was athletic and masculine, Terrence was artistic and a tad femi-nine. Somehow, though, they connected. There were times in college when Rick had felt like an outsider around the two of them-but then, Rick always felt like an outsider.

"No, thanks," Rick declined. "What are you doing, drinking so early-and in the yard, no less?"

"David and I have been doing this for the past two weeks. You're not the only newbie on the street."

"Oh, yeah?"

"A big muscle man," Terrence moaned. "He runs by here every day. Just moved into a house down the street. Yummy! He was in the military." His eyes lit up with mischief.

"Oh, I think I saw him. Almost caused me to run off the road."

"Uh-huh," Terrence said, sipping his drink. "Speaking of you and the road, are you supposed to be driving? Isn't that dangerous with the whole Cycloptic thing going on?"

Rick took a playful swipe at his friend's cheek. "You're the dangerous one," he joked, as best he could.

His attention, though, was immediately drawn to a grey Hummer pulling into the driveway behind his Festiva. The bass thumped loudly, shaking win-dows down the street before it was silenced.

"Who is this?" he inquired, awestruck by the massive vehicle.

"Hmmm?" Terrence said, as he turned to look at the land yacht. "Oh. It's just David."

"David owns a Hummer?"

"Of course not! That's his boyfriend's."

"Ricky!" David's voice called from behind the passenger-side door as it opened. He struggled to get out of the beast without falling awkwardly to the ground. "My God! Ricky! How are you?" he yelled as he ran to his friend with arms wide.

David had clearly been to the gym recently. His arms were twice the size they once were. He'd been a wrestler all through high school and college, but he had never looked as swollen.

"I'm good, David. How are you?" Rick smiled.

"Oh, you know," he shrugged off the question. "I'm so glad you're going to live with us! And if that Coby or any of his gambling goons tries to come around here, we'll sic Cliff on them."

"Cliff?"

Rick's question was answered as he saw the owner of the Hummer, a solid man built from muscle and veins, walking toward them in a pair of jeans and a t-shirt, both of which were barely able to contain the bulges beneath.

"Rick, this is my boyfriend, Cliff," David said with pride.

Cliff held out his huge hand with a square-jawed grin. "Hey there, Rick," he said with a deep baritone of a voice.

"Hi," Rick replied, taking the giant's hand. "You're huge."

"Eh … it's the steroids," Cliff admitted, nonchalantly.

"Oh." Was that supposed to lessen the wonder?

"Cliff, would you take Rick's things inside?" David asked.

"You bet," Cliff said.

He opened the Festiva's back door, nearly tearing it from its hinges, and got almost the entire lot of clothing and CDs with one muscled embrace. He walked to the house with heavy strides as the three friends watched by the car.

"Where did you find him?" Rick inquired.

"Becky Ridgeworth, down the street," David answered. "She knows a lot of guys in the film biz."

"He's an actor? I think I would remember if I saw him in anything. What has he been in?"

"You haven't seen him in anything, believe me," Terrence cut in, taking a break from the margarita. "You don't watch porn."

"He's a porn actor?" Rick glanced at David with eyebrows raised. It was as exclamatory as he ever got.

David grinned widely and nodded. "Becky does copy writing for porn studios … on the sly, of course."

"That's amazing. I imagine it's hard to breathe with that much man on top of you during sex, huh?" Rick winked.

"Oh, honey. Cliff's a bottom," David corrected.

Rick nearly fell over.

"Are you all right?" Terrence asked.

"Uh, yeah." Rick steadied himself. "Depth perception," he said, blaming his one eye. "Screws me up, that's all."

Cliff strode back out to the Festiva to retrieve the last bit of luggage. As he leaned into the backseat, Rick watched the muscular, steroid-enhanced ass.

"I'll have that drink now," he whispered to Terrence.

"So, did you see?" Melinda asked Cassie Bloom. "Another one of those boys has moved into that house. I just bet there's a whole gang there. Can you imagine the depravity?"

She sat in her custom kitchen island with a hot cup of expensive coffee in her hand. She insisted on having only the best. So what if it came out of a monkey's patootie in some African country? She had seen it on Oprah, and if it was good enough for Oprah, it was good enough for her.

"I don't know what decent folk are to do."

"Melinda," Cassie offered. "It's not the end of the world." Cassie's voice was a powerful thing, yet every word she spoke held a hint of sarcasm. "I rather like the Boys." She had referred to her young gay neighbors as 'the Boys' ever since she had met them. She had felt an immediate maternal affection for them.

"Uh-uh. Not me, Cassie," Melinda defended her position. "The neighborhood is positively going downhill. Why, just today that young man who inherited the Granger place ..."

"James."

"Yes, James. Well, he came running past my house as naked as the Lord made him!"

Cassie rather enjoyed the new young man's shirtless jogs, though telling this to Melinda would surely elicit a gasp of horror. "Melinda, darling, I saw him. He was wearing a pair of running shorts. Hardly dangerous."

There was that sarcasm. How Melinda hated it! And Cassie didn't seem to be enjoying her coffee either, swirling it with her spoon.

"Barely," Melinda muttered. She took a drink from her Ten Commandments mug, looking off into space.

Without all her money, which was left to her by a husband who died *very* mysteriously, Cassie would be nothing more than an immoral woman with short, masculine, blonde hair. But Melinda did love being seen with her. There was clout to the Bloom name all over town. Before his disappearance, Jackson Bloom held a high, secretive government position which paid him very handsomely.

"What are you afraid of, Mel?" Cassie mused, taking in the steam from her beverage.

"Patrick!" Melinda shot back, as if Cassie should know very well what she was afraid of. "Those boys and their effect on Patrick."

"Patrick's seventeen."

"He's still very impressionable, Cassie." She set her mug down with a thunk. "I know my own son. I walked into the living room just yesterday, and there he was sitting there watching a soap opera, and it had two boys kissing. Two boys, Cassie!" Her eyes widened as if seeing the image for the first time. "I don't mind him watching those shows, but I draw the line when they start advertising ... *homosexuals*," she whispered.

Cassie tried her best to stifle a laugh. "So, you're fine with him watching the greed, envy, adultery, and murder on those shows, as long as they don't have ... *homosexuals*," she mimicked. She smiled, shaking her head.

"We're Christians, Cassie, good Christians. That's all I'm saying." She sipped from her mug, clearly perturbed and hurt. How could Cassie not understand? She had a son, after all.

Cassie leaned over and took her hand. "I'm sure your son will be just fine," she comforted. Her eyes glanced to the wooden crucifix clock on the wall. Christ, hanging around, wasting time.

"How's your son?" Melinda asked.

"Jason's fine," Cassie answered, caught off guard.

"Are you on speaking terms again? He doesn't still blame you for his father's ... disappearance, does he?" Melinda pried.

"Dear God," Cassie sighed, eyes still on the cross. "We'll be fine, Melinda. Thanks for your concern, though."

"Well, what kind of friend would I be?" Her smile was a shade too pleasant.

The doorbell rang, freeing Cassie of the conversation. Melinda rose, still smiling, and walked daintily out of the kitchen to the front door.

"Howdy!" Cassie heard Becky Ridgeworth's booming voice.

Cassie grinned. Melinda was wildly disapproving of Becky. She did, after all, have dealings in that icky business of pornography.

"Becky," Cassie could hear Melinda groan. "What a nice surprise. Won't you come in?"

"Don't worry, Melinda," Becky said. "I'm just here for Cassie ... Cassie!" she hollered over Melinda.

"Coming!" Cassie responded from the kitchen. She set down her mug, flipped off the crucifix, and walked from the room.

"Becky!" She said, smiling. They embraced as if they hadn't seen one another in years.

"We need to add someone to the list for the party," Becky said excitedly. She was a round little woman in her mid-thirties, her hair always tied back in a ponytail, and her cheeks always red. Cassie liked it that Becky never put on any airs. While most the women in the neighborhood strutted about trying to mask their own shortcomings, Becky let them all hang out. She was perfectly at home in sweats and worn tennis shoes.

"Party?" Melinda inquired, staring from one to the other.

Who?" Cassie asked Becky, ignoring the question posed by Melinda.

"Rick Cooper," Becky explained. "He's the one with the eye patch who's moving in with Terrence and David today. He's a cutie!"

"Eye patch, huh?" Cassie gleamed. "Now, there's got to be an interesting story there."

"Party?" Melinda reiterated, emphasis in her expression.

"Well … yes, dear," Cassie finally answered, moving out the door to stand by Becky.

"You wouldn't want to come," Becky assured her.

"I might!" Melinda said with exasperation at the presumptuous and chubby woman.

Becky shrugged. "Ask her then," she said to Cassie.

"All right then." Cassie folded her arms. "Melinda, would you like to attend my gay porn party?"

Melinda's face dropped to the floor and Becky broke into laughter.

"Porn party?"

"I told you," Becky gasped in between guffaws.

"It won't be for a few weeks, but you're more than welcome to stop by if you want," Cassie said, touching Melinda's arm. "I'll talk to you later, hon."

Melinda watched as the two women walked down her driveway, Becky still giggling hysterically.

"Why do you even come over here?" Becky asked, as they walked down the sidewalk. "You know what she says about you, right?"

"That I murdered Jackson. Yes, I know."

"Then why."

"Amusement, my dear," Cassie explained. "And the fact that, deep down inside, I think Melinda Gold is just as warped as the rest of us. For God's sake, she just served me monkey-butt coffee. The woman is damaged."

She smiled, putting her arm around Becky's shoulder as they walked.

Steve had no idea how to tell Sandy the news. His stomach hurt at the thought of letting her down. He drove for an hour before finally turning onto Jasper Lane, Nick Drake crooning "Pink Moon" on the CD player to soothe his nerves. How could he let her down like this? And just when the next few months were going to be so busy! Sandy had already spent quite a bit of money on the decor and food for their annual July 4th costume party. (Why it was a costume party, Steve never quite understood.) She loved the tradition, and he had always found it rather enjoyable as well. But he was jobless now, let go that morning, and the money spent on the party suddenly seemed a waste.

"Fuck!" he whispered through a smile as Sandy stood on the porch, welcoming him home. She always managed to look gorgeous for him at the end of the day, her long brown hair shiny and perfect, her smile casual and loving, with no hint of worry. It would make telling her all the more difficult.

He glanced at himself in the rearview mirror. His dark hair was mussed a little from his nervous habit of running his fingers through it.

"Hey, baby!" she greeted as he got out of the car, reaching for his briefcase in the passenger seat. She walked to him and kissed him gently. "Hard day?" she asked, sensing trouble.

She ran her hands over his broad chest, patting down a bump in his tie. He had been a football player in college and still lifted heavily whenever he could. He had found a well-versed workout partner in David, from across the street.

"Uh, hon," he said, swallowing his guilt. "Let's have a seat on the porch."

He led her by hand to the pair of wicker chairs. He couldn't look at her, but stared somberly at the wood floor. "I don't know how to say this …"

"Just say it, baby. What's wrong?" Her smile had disappeared. Steve held her hands in his lap. "As long as you're not screwing somebody else, we'll be fine," she joked.

"Well, then we're fine," Steve assured her. "I've been laid off. The firm is folding."

Her face froze. "What? How could—I mean, Steven, we just spent all that money on the party."

"I know, baby."

"What will we do?" But she saw his desperation and disappointment in himself. It was no time to revel in doubt. She calmed herself and massaged his hands. "It will be okay, Steven."

"Yeah," he agreed out of necessity. "How will it?"

"It just will. It will. You'll see," she smiled. "Let's just focus on the party, okay? We can think about all this later."

"You still want to go through with the party?"

"Yes. Now more than ever".

He kissed her again. "I love you," he whispered.

Patrick stood with the refrigerator door open. His food choice was minimal, even though the shelves were fully stocked. It was mostly filled with the elegant but unexciting foods his mother insisted on preparing. That left him with two choices: cold pizza or cold fried chicken.

"Don't just stand there with the door open. Pick something," Melinda chided for the hundredth time.

He drew out the plate of foil-wrapped chicken and shut the door with a slam. Melinda shook her head as she prepared supper. "You'll ruin your appetite," she said.

"I don't like lemon chicken," Patrick responded. "I like my fowl fried and cold." He ripped at a chicken leg like a famished caveman, chicken skin hanging from his mouth.

"Oh, Patrick! Manners!"

"Boy, you show your mother some respect," Nanna said as she crept into the room, holding to the walker that she used due to a fall a few weeks prior. She insisted the fall was Patrick's fault in some way, though it wasn't clear how. In truth, it had nothing to do with any negligence on Patrick's part at all. Weeks earlier, Melinda was actually considering letting Patrick hang out with some non-church-going youngsters a few blocks over. Nanna would not have that. So, while Patrick was at school Nanna snuck into his room, placed his skate board in the hallway, and deliberately injured herself. Patrick, of course, was blamed and any thoughts of her son's sense of responsibility vanished from Melinda's mind. Nanna was intent on setting the world on the righteous path and that began with her own family.

"Patrick, you should get your hair cut before Bible study this evening," Melinda said. "It's getting shaggy."

"And change," Nanna added. "You look like a hooligan!"

"I'm not going," Patrick replied, his mouth full of cold chicken. He didn't look at either of them, but studied the greasy leg in his hands.

Melinda stopped what she was doing and stared at him. "You most certainly are!"

"No, I'm not," he reinforced. "They're a bunch of fanatics and hypocrites. Fuck them."

"Patrick!" Melinda gasped. "Wait till your father gets home."

"Mom, I'm not going. That's final. I'm seventeen. I can make my own decisions. Stop treating me like a child." He wrapped the chicken up again and placed it back in the refrigerator.

As he closed the door, his face was met by the wrinkly smack of his grandmother's hand. "Don't you speak to your mother like that!" She leered at him viciously.

With her short black hair, bulging eyes, and peach turtleneck she looked somewhat like an uncircumcised penis. But that was only on her bad days. On her good days, she looked like an ancient turtle slowly coming out of its shell.

Patrick glanced at his mother, who was clearly shocked by the old woman's act of violence. He gave his grandmother a hateful stare and walked out of the kitchen to his room.

"That's what you need to do, girlie. Show him who's boss!"

"Oh, Mother," Melinda moaned, returning her attention to the lemon chicken. "I just don't know what to do with him. And Frank's so busy with work, he really can't do anything. It's all I can do to get him to mow the yard." She paused and smiled, reflecting. "He's so good with that yard." Still, his late nights were troubling. She hated to admit it, but she had married Frank in part to get away from her mother. Yet, here she was, in the kitchen alone with Nanna.

"Well, you just leave Patrick to me," Nanna said, wobbling a bit on her walker. "You may be afraid to touch him, but I'll smack the poop out of him if he gets too uppity. It never hurt you or your sister when you were growing up. And I have never seen a boy more in need of a good butt-beating than Patrick. He's an ungrateful little brat!"

She walkered herself to the Virgin Mary cookie jar. "Crap!" she grunted. "There are no mint cookies." She put the lid back on the jar in disgust.

"I'll be driving you to the doctor's office to discuss your, um, problem," Melinda offered a change in subject. "Frank won't be able to drive you, and I am not letting Patrick anywhere near the car."

"Smart girl," Nanna said. "It would be so much easier if I had some little vehicle of my own to get around."

"Like what?"

"I don't know. A golf cart or something."

"There's an idea," Melinda smiled, pounding the chicken. "You have some of the most interesting ideas."

"I'm going to go watch some TV," Nanna said, as she turned for the door. A loud ripping noise issued from her back end as she went. Melinda closed her eyes in slight disgust.

She couldn't wait until they were able to do something about Nanna's gas problem.

Rick had been appointed the main floor guest room, which was a converted sun room. The large windows were draped in long, flowing, white curtains which tumbled in bunched excess on the dark wood floor. A high ceiling allowed for a sizable bed with four posts that shot up like the corn from the musical *Oklahoma!* David had given Terrence free reign to furnish the room, and he had picked up little oddities and useless accents from antique shops. Terrence had placed an old birdcage here, a wagon-wheel coffee table there. Occasionally he would throw in a more modern hint of style he had picked up from watching Nate Berkus or Home and Garden TV.

The glass doors opened upon a garden walkway. There was a quaint table and chair set there in case breakfast in the garden was desired. That had rarely happened, though, because David was always sleeping in after a long night of writing, and Terrence was always nursing his hangover.

It was a much nicer room than the one in which Rick had previously lived with Coby. They had a nice place overlooking the beach at one time. But that was before Coby lost control of things, of his addictive personality. (Whose idea was it to make it *their money* in the first place?) After that, they had to move to a seedy one-bedroom apartment, infested with every type of critter that could be named, not the least of which were roaches so big they could have been considered pets. But Rick stood for it because he saw no other way.

Rick unpacked his clothes and CDs easily enough. It didn't take long. He had only one suit to hang, a few button-ups, t-shirts, undies, and jeans. His music he lined up in order of likeability on the CD rack the Boys had generously provided. They had remembered his love of music from college. Emmylou Harris, Mary Chapin-Carpenter, Aimee Mann …

As he sat cross-legged on the floor in his socks, surrounded by CDs, he heard high-pitched banshee screams that were instantly recognizable as an overwrought Terrence. Rick opened his door and peered out to see what the problem was. David was standing in his Ginch Gonch boxer briefs with his arms folded. Terrence sat on the sofa wearing a look of absolute fear. He clutched at a purple-fringed pillow and rocked like a medicated psych patient.

"How did he find me?" Terrence squealed. "How in the world did he find me, David?"

"Maybe she told him," David posited in his most calming voice. "Have you given any thought to the Zoloft?"

"Fuck Zoloft!" Terrence hissed. "Tessa wouldn't dare tell him. She wouldn't!" He paused. "Would she?"

"Would she, what?" Rick asked, coming out of the door frame. "What's going on?"

"Terry here got a call," David explained. "Seems a ghost from his past wants to make contact."

"How did he find me?" Terrence whined again. "I have to move. I'm going to have to move, that's all there is to it. I'll have to go on the run! Like a fugitive, like Harrison Ford!"

"Yeah, you're just like Harrison Ford," David quipped, tongue-in-cheek. "Don't freak out."

"Thanks for your compassion," Terrence pouted. "I need a 'tini. Go make me a drink, would you, Ricky?"

"Alcohol won't solve a thing, Terry. The problem will still be there, plus you'll have a hangover to deal with," David chided, sitting down beside his frightened friend.

How many times had Rick seen this scene? In college, it was a weekly ritual. David comforting Terrence after some closeted jock had dropped him.

"I'm in such deep shit," Terrence moaned. He took the pillow and fell back, mimicking smothering himself.

"What?" Rick asked. "What is it? Are you in trouble with the law?"

"No, sweetie, nothing like that," David answered. "The whore got a call from his son."

Rick's mouth dropped. "Your son?"

"Yes!" Terrence yelled, throwing the pillow across the room. "I was sixteen and trying to convince myself I was straight. I just did it once with a girl named Tessa. Who knew I had such strong swimmers?"

"Oh, my God!" Rick said, working up some emotion for the phrase. He sat down in the recliner, leaning forward over his knees.

"I know, right?" Terrence concurred. He spit out a piece of fuzz from the pillow that had gotten into his mouth. "The bitch didn't even tell me she was pregnant. Shit," he moaned on the verge of tears. "I'm a bad father!" He fell into David's arms.

Rick shook his head in shock.

"Can I get that drink, sweetie?" Terrence asked Rick again.

Rick rose and was about to oblige.

"Ricky, don't do it," David warned. "He's got to face it. It won't do him any good to hide behind alcohol."

"You're such a bitch!" Terrence hissed.

"And you're a whore," David countered. "That's what got you into this."

"So," Rick intervened. "What's he like? Does he sound like you?"

"He sounds nice enough," Terrence sobbed. "His name's Christian. Can you believe that? Christian! That bitch named him that just to get back at me! I know it!"

"Oh," David grinned, patting him on the shoulder.

"He's seventeen now, and he says he would like to talk to me. You know, get a relationship going."

"And?" David asked.

"Well, if he calls I guess I have no choice. I'm already a deadbeat dad. I don't want to go any higher on the asshole list."

"Wow," David mused.

"What?" Tissue to the eyes and nose.

"You've made it, hon. You're a daddy."

CHAPTER 2

As a new morning cast its light over the pleasant, harmonious tones of the peaceful neighborhood of Jasper Lane, Melinda had risen with a satisfying stretch and yawn. It could have been a perfect day.

She had gotten dressed in casual but stylish clothes, combed her soft hair lovingly, and had her expensive coffee, ready to take on whatever challenges or miracles the Lord might give her. So what if Frank was already gone by the time Melinda felt the touch of morning's light? He was a busy man, a very busy man.

Still, and she thought this to herself with a pang-more like a pinch-in her heart, she wished he were home more often. Why was he always needed at work? Other women would be suspicious, but Melinda knew he was a Christian man. He had no need to turn to other women. She was happy to do her duty as a wife any time he would ask. Theirs had never been a particularly passionate marriage, but if he wanted more of her, all he ever needed to do was ask. She was thankful to him anyway for taking her away from Nanna, at least for a while. He was a Christian man, yes. They were a Christian family put together before God. They were above the carnality of the rest of the world—adulterers, homosexuals, Muslims, and Mormons.

She had walked outside, ready to face her day, a slight discomfort from the thoughts churning in her head dimming her smile just a bit. Then she saw him again, all six feet of him. She knew she would be unable to speak. She had promised herself the day before that she would confront him, but the same queer feeling came over her again. Why, she felt as if she would burst into flames!

Quickly, she ducked back inside and peeked out the window as James Something-or-other sprinted down the street. She had fallen into lust! She knew it. Something had to be done for the safety of her own soul.

She could make it a point to miss him every morning, but that would just be selfish. There were weaker souls in the neighborhood who were certainly lusting after him as well. But was she truly responsible for them too? Was she to be an instrument of righteousness?

Realizing she could not in any way bring herself to talk to the man, Melinda decided the right course of action would be a letter. A polite but firm note written on her best scented stationary and delivered to him by hand would be best. Then she would smile and walk away.

But wouldn't that be rude? Just to hand a stranger a letter and then walk away with not a word? That would be very suspicious.

Perhaps, then, she would simply place it in his mailbox. No need to send it through the post. After all, he just lived down the street. Besides, placing the letter personally felt so much more upstanding.

She smiled at her decision, and walked to the roll-top desk in the living room.

"How to start?" she asked herself, twirling her favorite fine-point pen between her fingers.

Dear Sir, Melinda wrote, the pen gliding elegantly across the beautiful blue sheet of her eighth-and-hopefully-final draft. It was a shame she did not know his last name.

You most likely are unfamiliar with me. My name is Melinda Gold. My family and I live just down the street.

I dearly hope you are finding your new home and neighbors pleasant. It is of the utmost importance that we, as a neighborhood, provide a welcoming and comfortable environment for all. I'm sure you would agree. After all, I have heard that you were a military man, so you must, of course, realize there are social norms that must be upheld for any society to thrive. The well-being of all depends on it.

It is precisely for this reason that I am writing you. You see, every morning, as I tend to my lawn (which, I am sure, you have noticed, is the most austere and well-kept on the block), I see you out jogging. Now, mind you, I have nothing against one staying healthy. Far from it! The Lord says that the body is a temple, and so it is. We should all strive to care so deeply for ourselves. God gave us these wonderful vessels as gifts, and you have crafted yours most exquisitely.

But you see, this is a good, clean, Christian street. To have someone running around only half-dressed … well, I'm afraid it just doesn't look right. I personally have no problem with it. I'm simply thinking of the children. They are very impressionable at such young ages, especially the boys. As a Christian yourself, I'm sure you understand.

Anyway, I sincerely hope this letter finds you well! Feel free to drop in anytime! Don't be a stranger.

Melinda Louise Gold

"Yoo-hoo!" Becky Ridgeworth whistled as she walked into the Jones' backyard.

Sandy lay out on her back on a beach towel, soaking up rays of light. She wore only the tiny pink bottoms of her swimsuit. The top lay beside her. Her large breasts were as tan as the rest of her.

"Hi, Becky," Sandy replied, casually. She didn't even open her eyes.

"Sandy, honey," Becky said. "You are the only woman gal enough to lay about with your teats exposed."

"I suppose everyone in the neighborhood has seen them. It's not a big deal to me."

"Nor should it be, darlin'. Those are some nice hooters." She approached Sandy for a closer look. "My, your aureoles are huge!"

Sandy couldn't help but smile. "What do you need, sweetie?" she asked.

"I'm just bringing this basket of tablecloths over for Cassie."

She held a large basket full of Cassie's finest linens.

"Oh!" Sandy said, sitting up with excitement. Her breasts bounced in unison. "For my Fourth party! Yay! Tell her I said thanks so much!"

"I'll just set them down over here," Becky said, placing the basket on a lawn chair. "I have to get back to work. I'm on my lunch hour. Toodles!"

Sandy kept staring at the basket full of good, strong fabric long after Becky had left. Her joy soon turned to guilt. Here she was, sunning herself topless in the backyard, readying for a party, while Steve was out pounding the pavement, desperately searching for a job to keep them afloat.

She lay back on the ground, trying to think of some way to be useful. Was she just an ornament now? Her mother had been a strong woman, a college professor, and that was always Sandy's plan too. But that was before she met Steve. Now she felt like she was some remnant of the past; a pretty and sweet housewife, her husband's pride and joy. His show pony. The strange thing was, though, that she rather liked it.

She had mentioned getting a job to make things easier, and while Steve nodded in support, Sandy knew his pride was hurt by the suggestion. He saw himself as a failed provider.

Sandy sighed and grabbed her bikini top and towel. She carried them back inside with the basket.

David stretched, popping his neck, as he descended the stairs from his room wearing just his boxer briefs. It had been a good, solid morning of writing. His new article for *Gay Men's Fitness* would be done by the time of the Fourth party.

In the kitchen, he stood in front of the opened refrigerator. His eyes studied the contents until he settled on a bottle of flavored sparkling water. He opened it and took a long drink.

Shutting the door, he heard Terrence call from the living room. As he entered, he saw Rick staring toward the recliner with an expression of befuddlement.

"What's up, Terry?" David asked.

"How do I look?" Terrence asked from the recliner.

"Yeah, David. How does he look?" Rick echoed with dry humor in his tone.

Terrence sat lounging back, his legs crossed at the ankles, with a newspaper opened to the Sports section in his hand. He wore an orange and brown argyle sweater, beneath which was a starchy white dress shirt. His dark brown corduroy pants were rolled up at the bottom, and his feet were covered by argyle socks and rich brown loafers. In his mouth was an unlit pipe and he read the paper through faux, black-rimmed spectacles.

"Um," David stumbled out. "What were you going for?"

"A father. Do I look like a father? This is how a father would dress, right?"

David looked at Rick, who snickered in response.

"I don't think there's a rule book for how dads dress."

"I'm not kidding, guys," Terrence defended. "I'm a father now. I've got to start perpetuating that image. You know? PTOs, Take Your Son to Work Day, meeting college recruiters … I have to look respectable."

"Terry, you just heard from him yesterday. I think you might want to slow down a little."

"Absolutely not! Too much time has been lost already." Terrence clumsily rose from the recliner. The lever stuck and he almost tipped the chair. He got to his feet as the recliner fell back with a thud. He stood straight, adjusting his crooked glasses and nearly gagging on the pipe. "PTOs, David! Father/son day, Rick! I'm going to be there for him from here on out."

"Terrence, just be yourself," David suggested. "That's all a son can ask for."

"I will be myself, bitch! This is me bettering myself. So, you're just going to have to deal with it!" He threw the paper to the floor with a huff, and stormed dramatically from the room.

"Dammit, these fatherly clothes are itchy!" he complained as he squirmed his way to his room.

"PTOs?" Rick said. "Take Your Son to Work Day? Doesn't he need to have a job first?"

David shrugged helplessly and drank the remainder of the water in one swig.

Rick put the ipod Terrence loaned him on "shuffle" and set out on a walk. Jasper Lane didn't look that scary after all, he noted. In fact, it was very pleasant. The tall trees provided shade all the way down the street, birds sang, bees buzzed. One buzzed too close and Rick swatted ferociously for a moment, but then regained his cool.

No, it might not be bad at all living with David and Terrence on Jasper Lane. It had to be better than where he had come from. Coby had been a mistake that had cost him many things. A mistake that began with their meeting at a bar where Coby had been playing pool and ended with Rick losing an eye from a knife jab intended for Coby. As Rick stood behind his boyfriend trying to defuse a desperate situation, Coby ducked at just the right-or wrong-moment.

But it was more serene here. Rick persuaded himself to keep his mind on the present, particularly the relaxing afternoon environment.

As he passed the Gold residence, the young son, Patrick, looked to be quite miserable. He sat on the porch steps, his eyes looking through Rick at some distant dream. Mrs. Gold—Melinda, he had been told—came out and said something. Rick couldn't quite make out what that "something" was, but she didn't look happy. She had that motherly glare of disapproval.

Rick walked onward to the beat of some club anthem. It wasn't his style of music, but it would do. Music of any kind was food for the soul, if there be souls.

Steve Jones passed Rick, offering a wave. He pulled into his drive and his wife, Sandy, rushed out to meet him. They were so cute. An all-American couple that was so perfect in every way. They almost seemed like cardboard cutouts. They reminded Rick of the paper dolls his sister had played with as a kid. They seemed as static and flat.

No, that was mean. He shook the thought from his head and walked past. Besides, there was a hint of some discouragement on Steve Jones' face. Surely they had problems just like everyone.

The dance grooves in his ears almost made it impossible to hear the car horn being blown at him. He removed the ear pieces as Cassie Bloom rolled up beside him in her shiny red BMW. She lowered the window and smiled. Rick nodded as he walked closer to the vehicle. The coolness of an air-conditioned breeze wafted toward him.

"Can I give you a ride?" she said.

"No, thanks. I just moved in yesterday, so I'm taking a walk to get to know the neighborhood."

"I'm Cassie Bloom," she offered. "Now you know me. You must be Rick. The Boys told me you were coming. I'm so sorry I haven't been over to introduce myself and welcome you."

"It's no problem," Rick assured her. "I was pretty tired anyway."

Cassie accepted this graciously. "You should come to the club sometime," she said.

"Club?"

"That's where I'm headed now. My friend Vera owns it. It's where all the cute gay boys can be found." She winked knowingly.

"I'm not one for clubs." He was trying to be polite.

"Well, then, come over to my place."

"Sure," Rick agreed.

"Promise?"

"Sure."

Cassie nodded. "Well, I'll let you get back to your discovering. I'm late anyway." she began to drive off. "Remember, you promised," she said.

Rick, finally freed of discomfort from the encounter, put his ear-pieces on once again. Near the end of Jasper Lane, just before Ms. Bloom's fine palace, Rick passed the home of the military man. The three car garage was opened and he was arranging boxes, lawn equipment, and bags of mulch. Sweat rings showed in dark semi-circles under his arms on his tight, grey army shirt. When the man glanced in Rick's direction, Rick quickly focused his attention on the aloe plant on the porch.

Rick remembered he had tried his hand at taking care of an aloe plant once. He was quite proud of himself for the first month, until he'd had to go on a business trip for a few days. Having Coby take care of it wasn't the best decision he had ever made. Coby's idea of plant care was urinating in the soil whenever his bladder got too full from drinking beer. The plant died soon after Rick returned home. There were so many foreign chemicals in Coby's system that the plant was poisoned from the toxicity.

James Tucker piled the last box of his Uncle Willie Granger's possessions in a corner. Someday he might throw them away or sell them. They really had no meaning anymore. But to do that right away just felt disrespectful somehow.

He wiped the sweat from his forehead and closed the garage doors. His plan for the night was relaxation. He'd grab a beer from the fridge and sit out on the porch where he could play his guitar in the old rocking chair. He was good, too, for a beginner.

The doors closed, he turned to walk back into the house. As he did so, he stepped on a yellowed photograph that had fallen from one of the boxes. Leaning down to pick it up, he saw that it was Willie and another young man. Their arms were interlocked, and they smiled contentedly as they sat on a fallen tree trunk. They appeared to be in their late twenties. Strong, healthy young men in strange, very proper attire. James was sure the man his uncle was posing with was his partner, his lover. There was just that certain look between them. Desire fulfilled and completely living up to expectation.

Willie had left behind many ghosts of his past adventures in the forms of pictures of friends and lovers in photo albums and framed in simple casements. He always looked so happy in his pictures, as if the bigotry of others hadn't affected him at all.

James was about to return the photo to its box, but then decided against it. Instead, he would hang it on the refrigerator door. The house still needed his uncle. And James found that he needed to be reminded of his uncle's hidden normalcy.

Patrick Gold lay asleep, twisted in the sheets like the truth from a politician's mouth. Night had fallen and he was once again having a dream directed and written by John Hughes.

He walked into his school's library, except all the books on the shelves had blue covers and the librarian behind the desk was not an elderly lady or a gruff, portly man. No, instead there stood a vision, a beauty, a blessed angel sent down to purge the world of the evil that was his family. He realized it was the girl who had sat in front of him in Biology last semester. She never noticed him then, but she saw him now.

She licked her lips in a seductive, bad-rap-video way and he drew closer. He wasn't nervous. This was their regular meeting, an agreed-upon rendezvous.

He leaned in to kiss her cherry red lips, but suddenly the girl transformed into something hideous. Nanna stood before him, still wearing the bright lipstick and halter top.

"What are you leering at, boy?" she cracked.

Patrick awoke, drenched in sweat and terror. He was sure he had screamed as well. He reached for the remote and turned on the television.

"Something happy," he whispered to himself. "Find something happy or sexy. *Baywatch* or *Barney*."

CHAPTER 3

James Tucker inspected the tin of processed tuna. It certainly didn't look like it should cost as much as it did, but then, he had been far from civilian life for some time. Military life was easier in some respects. He didn't necessarily have to go shopping as much, for one. It was a good thing half of the items in his basket had recipes on their packaging or he might never eat anything but fast food burgers and Chinese take-out. No, that was a lie. He would never eat so carelessly. At least, not on a regular basis. He was too health-conscious for that.

He sighed and tossed the tuna into the cart, where it landed with a thud on the pile of packaged steaks. Slow, manipulative music played quietly overhead as James made his way, dressed in a green t-shirt, khaki shorts, and flip-flops, down the chilly store aisle. His eyes glazed over cans of various products, though he didn't really stop to look at anything in particular. Nothing was catching his attention. It all looked the same, and much too expensive, though cost was not necessarily a problem anymore. After all, his late uncle, Willie Granger, had left him not only his rather nice home, but also a sizeable sum of money.

Willie was perceived as a somewhat creepy old man. He kept to himself for the most part, except for a few stray cats near the end, but he liked James. James never understood why until he discovered a kinship to the old man on more than familial terms after rummaging through his uncle's things. Willie, as explained by love letters and ancient pictures, had a lover at one point, a male lover. James understood then, and the letters became night-time reading. It suddenly became even more regretful that James had not bothered to get to know his uncle better.

Willie was found dead one afternoon by a passing Jehovah's Witness. He had collapsed in the doorway, asphyxiated from an unfortunate allergy to felines.

In any event, James was three weeks settling into the big house-sans cats-and trying to find a new life outside of the United States military. The hardest part was meeting people. He was never any good at it, the introductions. The closest he had come was his daily greetings with the woman with the nice lawn. Melinda, he thought her name was. But when he passed she would just gawk at him as if she wanted to say hello … or something. She made him more than a little uneasy.

Then there were the two who watched him run by every afternoon, David and … Terrence, yes, that was it. Terrence. There was no mistaking what was on their minds as they drank margaritas in their lawn chairs.

James laughed, almost affectionately, at the thought of them. He had to admit he liked their attention more than that of the lawn lady. They were at least upfront about it.

He picked up a bag of pasta and compared it to another. Which was the better choice? Was there a difference? One looked thinner than the other. Did that matter?

The only people he had met on Jasper Lane outright, who had introduced themselves to him, were Cassie Bloom, who resided in the massive house on the cul de sac, and her cheerful friend, Becky Ridgeworth. They were both amiable enough, and Cassie had invited him, rather flirtatiously, to some type of movie party later in the summer.

"Keep your schedule clear," she had cooed with a wink.

Steve and Sandy Jones had also invited him to their Fourth of July costume party, whatever that was. They were a pleasant, perfectly All-American couple. The costume party was actually the reason James had ventured out to the stores in the first place. Although he couldn't believe it had arrived so quickly, it was already the Fourth and he still had no costume. On his way to accomplishing that mission, he thought he might also get some grocery shopping done.

The costume conundrum was ever on his mind, even as he thumped melons for ripeness. Did he have to dress up? Was it required? He hadn't gone anywhere in costume since grade school. What did grown men wear to costume parties?

He settled on a cantaloupe, and then grabbed a small watermelon too. Why the hell not?

Glancing up, he recognized the man with the eye patch who had moved in with David and Terrence the previous week. He hadn't heard his name yet, but he was certainly attractive. The eye patch made him seem vulnerable. Damaged, even.

Should he introduce himself? He had been wanting to do so. Did people do that? Did grown men do that? In the fruit section of the local grocery store?

Before he could get any answers from himself, the vulnerable, eye patch-wearing stranger disappeared. James took it as a sign. Besides, it was getting on in the morning, and he needed to go find some sort of costume.

What the hell does a grown man wear to a costume party?

"I'm back!" Rick called as he walked into the house with bags of groceries in both arms.

David jumped from the couch in his boxers, where he was reading the latest edition of *Hot Gay Men's Fitness*. Flinging the magazine onto the apothecary/coffee table, he freed Rick's arms of one of the bags. Rick wondered if he owned more than a couple pairs of pants or shirts. All he ever wore were his underwear. Of course, as a writer working from home, what need did he have to get dressed? Plus, David did have an athletic build. He was doing a public service by staying so scantily clad.

"There's more in the car," Rick said as they made their way to the kitchen.

"I'll get it," David offered, racing out the door and returning just as quickly, a natural athlete.

"Where's Terry?" Rick asked. He immediately began unpacking boxes and cans.

"On the phone with Christian. They've been talking all morning." He dug into a bag and found his whey protein. "Yes! Thanks!" he said.

"Not a problem," Rick responded. "They've been talking a lot the last week. Sounds like a nice relationship is forming."

"Yeah, and it's about time."

"How do you mean?"

"Terry needs to find some kind of solid relationship, you know? He's got me, but that's about it."

"No family? I know he hasn't had any long-term boyfriends?" Rick tossed a jar of jalapeños across the island for David to put in the cupboard.

"Nope," David said. "His family was never too close, and Terry is more of a hook-up guy when it comes to men?"

"Hmmm. Well, he seems to be adjusting to the news well enough."

"Seems," David stressed the word. "I'm sure something will happen soon to freak him out. Just wait."

"Shit!" came a cry from somewhere in the house.

"See," David sighed.

Terrence rushed into the kitchen looking agitated.

"What now?" David inquired.

"He wants to meet!" Terrence squealed. "My little renegade sperm wants to meet me!"

"So?" Rick asked. "That's great, right? You can get to know him now."

"No, it's not great," Terrence hissed. "I can't keep who I am hidden for the duration of a stay."

"What?"

"Terrence has been butching his voice up," David explained.

"You mean Christian doesn't know you're gay?"

Terrence shook his head and seated himself at the island, head in hands, fingers massaging his shaved scalp.

"I don't know," David interjected. "It's the silliest thing I've ever heard, that butch voice of yours. The kid's probably figured it out."

"Oh, shut up!" Terrence said, throwing a peach from the island centerpiece at David.

"I'm just saying," David replied, catching the fruit.

"Have you decided when and where you'll meet?" Rick asked.

"No. I don't even know if I'm going to do it."

"Of course you will," David said. "You need to meet him, Terrence. He's your kid. You need some type of family besides us."

"I know," Terrence agreed, his head hanging heavy. "Shit," he mumbled as his head fell with a thump to the island. Rick came up behind him, rubbing his back comfortingly.

"Just don't let it get you down," David consoled him. "Go fix us some margaritas and get everything ready. The *Show* starts soon. Rick, are you joining us on the lawn?"

"Uh, I don't think so," Rick replied. "But I'll be outside. It's a nice day to wash my car."

"Ricky, that car's a piece of crap. Washing it won't improve that," Terrence said, his head still buried.

"That's all right," Rick deflected. "And I need to find a costume for later."

"Yeah. There's another thing to look forward to," David posited to Terrence. "That hot UPS man is coming. Sandy invited him, and she told me he's coming as Batman. I know your fetish for superheroes. That's something, huh?"

Terrence lifted his head from the island. "Yeah," he griped. "It's something." A smile threatened the edges of his mouth.

Ah, Hot UPS Guy! Terrence had ordered from catalogs and online stores just to see the young man sauntering up their walkway in his cute shorts.

"It's something," he repeated, as they walked outside.

David and Terrence set up the lawn chairs as usual in the front yard, sporting their trendy shades and square-cut swim trunks. Before too long they both sat comfortably with drinks in hand.

"You know, you both look like every gay stereotype I think I've ever seen," Rick said as he prepared to wash his car in the driveway. It was a nice day for it. Jackie Green sang "Honey, I've Been Thinking About You" on the car CD player.

"Oh, blah!" Terrence shot back. "Who cares?" He took a small sip from the margarita he held.

"You should be more like us," David added. "Maybe you'd get a date."

Rick grinned, a slight tug on the corner of his mouth, and soaped up the beaten old car. But David had a point. Rick hadn't been out on a date in forever. It had been since before Coby, and it wasn't because he was less than attractive. He had, in fact, very striking features, eye patch-of-mystery aside. He just lacked the nerve to actually act on impulse. He let moments of possible intrigue flee from him, feeling that he was something less than special permeated his being. He knew that his escapades would never interest any of the ladies on Jasper Lane. He wasn't sure if that was a positive or a negative. The only thing that he was certain of was that he would not find his name mentioned in the larger-than-life stories retold like punch lines at dinner parties and barbecues.

Terrence and David were more of the go-getter types. They were loved and their adventures legendary. There was hardly a night since Rick had arrived that there wasn't something going on ... or someone going down. And the Boys always seemed to get themselves in trouble for it.

"Get over here and relax!" Terrence said. "The Show's about to start." He spilled a drop of drink on his chest and David licked it off playfully. They both giggled like teenagers.

"*The Show*?" Rick asked. "Is that his name?"

Terrence and David whispered jokingly to each other before continuing with their sipping and sun-worshiping.

Rick lathered up the car, then began to rinse it with the hose. He didn't want to be robbed of seeing *The Show*, though. He had seen the man jogging around enough to understand the attraction. He'd even snuck a quick peek at him in the produce section at the grocery store earlier.

Suddenly, the temperature seemed to shoot up several degrees, the flowers almost drooping from the heat.

"There he is!" Terrence snickered excitedly, hitting David with childish jabs.

Rick looked up quickly. Sure enough, there he was, shirtless and sweating, each muscle twitching and flexing as he ran. Rick swallowed in embarrassed desire.

In all probability, anyone who was watching the ex-military man (and there were many) saw him in the same slow-motion movement, pectorals bouncing in fleshy waves. He wore military shorts, green and cut well above the knees so as to provide a better glimpse of his fine leg muscles.

David and Terrence panted and moaned, not so discreetly.

"My lord, those legs!" Terrence said.

"My god, that chest!" David answered.

Rick glanced at them and grinned, then returned to his task. That was good enough for today. Maybe tomorrow he could come up with some other plan to guarantee him a show.

He turned off the hose and began wiping the car down. It was streaking a bit, but he had time to wax it before heading to the party.

Prior to that, though, he would give himself a shower with the hose to wash off the lust.

Behind him, suddenly, the giddiness and cackling of his two boozing house-mates ceased. There was an odd quiet, as if someone was about to jump out and scream *"Boo!"* Rick turned around out of curiosity, and his heart threatened to leap from his chest.

In front of him stood the army man with his brawny, muscular hands placed on his brawny, muscular hips. A droplet of sweat fell from the handsome man's forehead; his hair was just beginning to grow back from its clipped military style.

"Hi," he said, breathing heavily. A gorgeous grin lay across his face. A face that was not as hard or stern as one might expect from a military man.

"Hi," Rick said, stunned.

Terrence and David watched, mouths agape, from the yard.

"Nice day for it," the man said, referring to the car wash. "My name's James. I'd shake your hand, but I'm all sweaty."

"That's okay," Rick said. "I'm Rick. I'm all moist ... wet! I'm all wet. A little sweat won't bother me." He held out his hand and James took it.

"So, listen, Rick. I've seen you around ... I've noticed you ..." He was stumbling to say something. "What I mean to say-and bear with me because I've been in the army and it's been a while-but I've seen you around and ... Would you like to go do something?"

"Now?" Rick asked, though he knew perfectly well what James was asking. "With *me*?"

"Yes ... no. Not now. Sometime, though."

"A date?"

"A date. Yes," James said. "I was planning on trying to strike up a conversation with you about the car and then gently slide into asking, but ... I was nervous-am nervous-so I just thought I'd get it over with ... So I'd know for sure right away, you know?"

"Uh, yeah." Rick shielded his eye patch self-consciously. "I'd love to. I'd like that very much. Are you sure? With me?"

"Yes. Absolutely, with you. Good." James sighed. The relief cascaded from him. He began to walk slowly backward with a victorious grin on his face, his arms swinging freely. "I'll catch you tonight at the party, okay? We can set it up then."

"Sounds good," Rick said, smiling in return.

James turned around with a slight, congratulatory hop. Though dazed, Rick couldn't help but check out his ass. It was clearly one of the best and most sculpted in the neighborhood, rivaling even David or Steve Jones.

James ran on down the street, waving once back at Rick, and then jogging out of sight. Gayhound caught sight of him and jogged alongside.

"You fucking bitch!" Terrence bellowed.

"He doesn't have to go anywhere," David complained playfully to Terrence. "They come to *him*!"

"You're going to tell us everything that happens," Terrence ordered. "*Everything*, Cinderella! Your stepsisters want to know."

"No way, boys," Rick replied. "This is going to stay quiet. You can't tell anyone. I don't want the whole neighborhood knowing."

"Too late," David said, as he raised his shades to see the portly figure of Becky Ridgeworth power-walking up the drive toward Rick, a look of curiosity on her plump face like a heat-seeking missile.

"Cassie Bloom probably already knows," David said. "You're the talk of Jasper Lane already."

"So, this it," Rick said to himself with a worrisome grin. "My ticket into absurdity."

"Ricky!" Becky hollered. "What news? What news?"

"What's your name again?" Nanna asked the tall black woman who sat opposite her and Melinda at the dining room table. Cassie Bloom sat beside the elaborately adorned woman. Coffee mugs with steaming beverages sat in front of them.

"Vera," came the deep-voiced reply. She smiled out of politeness. It was a big, broad smile. She wore a floppy straw hat with an orange scarf wrapped around it, and a matching orange blazer over a yellow blouse.

"Vera what?" Nanna pried suspiciously, her eyes squinting.

"Just Vera. Like Cher ... or Caligula."

"Vera's a close friend," Cassie explained. "A family friend."

"You're a big gal," Nanna observed.

"Mother!" Melinda chided.

"I take after my father," Vera said, then blew on her coffee before taking a sip.

"She's a gem," Cassie smiled.

"Aw," Vera cooed, placing a large hand on Cassie's.

Melinda felt awkward in the silence that followed. Nanna was still squinting at Vera, and Cassie was enjoying Melinda's uncomfortable shifting.

The silence was disturbed as Patrick walked into the room, hardly noticing the guests.

"Patrick," Melinda said. "Say hello to our guests. This is Cassie and her ... friend, Vera."

"Hey," Patrick mumbled. "Mom, I want to go out tonight," he said, changing the course of conversation.

"Oh, are you going to hang out with your Bible study group?" Melinda inquired, more as a prideful show than an earnest question.

"Uh, no. The Rikers down the street are having a thing for the Fourth."

"No," Melinda shot him down. "Absolutely not. The Rikers are not good people. The mother is a drunk and those children are out of control."

"Mom, come on! I want to spend some time outside of this place."

"You heard your mother!" Nanna interjected roughly.

"Patrick, we can discuss this later. We have company now."

"Discuss this!" he said, flipping her off. He rushed from the room, heading for the patio.

"Boy! You get back here! I'll tan your hide!" Nanna shouted, standing up as fast as she could. As she did so, a steady stream of flatulence escaped from her.

Cassie and Vera did little to conceal their surprise at the sudden outburst from Nanna.

"Oh, my!" Vera gasped with a laugh. "I second that!" Cassie broke into hysterics, hitting her friend playfully on the arm.

Melinda was wide-eyed and pale. "Look at the time, Mother!" she said. "We should be going. We want to get that shopping done before the stores close early for the holiday." She rose from the table.

"What?" Nanna said defensively. "It's just a little flatulence. Can't do nothing about it."

"You could stop drinking milk," Melinda grumbled under her breath. "Let's go, Mother." She pushed the older woman, who was now doing her best to get around without the walker. "Don't worry about the dishes. I'll get them when we get back. Can you show yourselves out?"

But she didn't wait for a response. She and Nanna were already out the door.

"That's one smelly old woman," Vera commented.

Cassie nearly fell from her chair.

Patrick lounged with his arms stretched behind his head in a chair by the pool in the backyard. Cassie and Vera slid open the door and stepped out onto the deck. It wasn't nearly as nice or as large as Cassie's own pool area. For all of Melinda's pretenses and appearances, Frank was still a working-class man. There was nothing wrong with that. It was just the way it was.

Cassie sat down on the chair opposite Patrick, leaning forward with her hands clasped. Vera stood sizing down the pool area.

"How are things, Patrick?" Cassie asked, a hint of natural concern in her voice.

"You saw," Patrick answered, staring at the blue water of the pool. "Mom doesn't have a freakin' clue that you're a dude, does she?"

Vera turned from studying the pool, realizing the question was posed to her. "I don't suppose she does, baby," she said, approaching a chair to sit.

"I didn't think so. She'd flip out."

"Doesn't seem to bother you so much," Vera commented.

"I like different things," Patrick shrugged. "There are so many interesting people in the world, but I won't meet any of them if my mom has her way."

"Well, there's your Bible study group," Cassie joked.

"They're dipshits," Patrick explained. "They're fine with not having any fun, it seems. They say God makes no mistakes, right? And then they go and say gay people, or whoever, are sinful and flawed. I don't get it."

"Are you gay, Patrick?" Cassie inquired.

"No. But sometimes I wish I was, just so I could piss her off."

"So, you don't do anything if it's not with this church group?"

"Nope. And that means I don't do anything, because I don't want to hang around with those fucks." He sat up, pulling his arms down and facing Cassie. "I want to date, you know? I just want to have fun like a normal teenager. Before I'm not a teenager anymore."

"Makes sense to me, sweetie," Cassie agreed.

"I can't even get a real job. She wants to know where I am all the time. It's pissing me off! If I made my own money I could save up and get out of here. I'd even apply to college, but Mom would never agree to pay for it. Bad association, she would say."

Cassie could see that it felt good for him to get his feelings off his chest. Had anyone ever asked him how he felt before?

"Would your mother allow you to get a job with someone she knew?"

"Maybe … I dunno," Patrick mumbled. He swept his bangs from his forehead. His hair was getting blonde highlights from the summer sun.

Cassie glanced at Vera, raising her eyebrow in contemplation.

"What are you thinking, Miss Cass?" Vera asked, knowing the look quite well.

"Patrick," Cassie began. "I have a pool, a very large one, which requires a lot of work. More work than I'm afraid I can do. I usually hire some professionals to take care of it weekly, but I would rather have someone I knew better, someone I trusted, you know?"

Patrick was eyeing her intently, taking every word in like it was the first time anyone had ever spoken directly to him.

"Would you like to be my pool boy, Patrick?" Cassie asked. "I'll pay you well … *very well.*"

Patrick's heart was beating wildly at the job prospect, at the idea of getting away from his mother for a few hours a week.

"Of course," Cassie smiled, "it would be a daily position. You might need to be over there from morning till night. It's a very big pool." She winked.

"Why, Patrick," Vera exclaimed, "I do believe you are smiling!"

"How about it, Patrick? Would your mother allow that?"

"Are you kidding?" he nearly shouted, eyes wide as saucers. "You're a friggin' social god to my mother!"

"Oh," Cassie said, feigning modesty.

The back yard was finally coming together. Steve had put up the lights the day before. Sandy had originally found some shaped like Lady Liberty, but they eventually opted for ordinary strands of red, white, and blue. The tables were set and decorated with various patriotic knick-knacks, and most of the food would be delivered within the hour. Steve also insisted on doing a little grilling. What was the Fourth without a cook-out?

Cliff had been over in the morning to help out with moving the tables around, doing most of the moving without Steve's help. He was so large he could pick up a table all by himself.

"It's the 'roids," he admitted when Sandy complimented him.

He and David would be over before the party got started to aid in getting the food prepared and set out. They were, after all, Steve and Sandy's mirror couple. They all played poker together every Wednesday night.

Steve was working on the sound system for the music, making sure all the wires were correctly connected so that the bass would be heard all over the neighborhood, when Sandy came outside.

"We should get into our costumes soon," Sandy suggested, straightening the edges of a table cloth.

"We've got time, I think," Steve replied, still very busy.

Sandy loved his attentiveness. Every detail would be perfect. He would make sure of it … for her. He knew how much she looked forward to the Fourth of July party every year.

He worked with his shirt off. Sweat dripped from his muscular arms and glistened in his dark chest hair. She was always very grateful to David for getting Steve back to the gym. His football player physique had started to fade after just a year out of college, but it was returning, thankfully, due to David's influence.

"You are going to have to take such a long shower," Sandy said, shaking her head.

He laughed as he tightened a wire onto the last speaker.

Sandy poured a tall glass of lemonade for him, and he took it graciously.

"Thanks, hon," he said, taking a big gulp that emptied the entire glass.

"How are we going to do this?" Sandy asked, concern once again evident on her face.

"We'll do it," Steve comforted. "We'll do it. That's all. We have a savings. We can live off that until I can find a new job."

"Steve, even when you do find another job, you're still not going to bring in as much as you were."

"What do you want me to do, Sandy?" he shot back, defensively.

She stared at him, surprised by his counter. "Nothing," she said gently, wiping a bead of sweat from his brow. "Let's not think about it. I'm sorry."

"No, babe," he replied, taking her hand and kissing it. "I'm sorry. I let you down."

"Steven Emory Jones!" she exclaimed. "You did no such thing. You have never let me down. Ever. As long as I'm with you, that's all I care about. We could move to a trailer park in the center of the Bible Belt and, as long as we're together, I'd be happy."

"Really?" Steve looked at her with a knowing grin.

"Well, I mean, we'd have to have the nicest trailer." She laughed and kissed him.

He embraced her playfully. "Now you need a shower, too!" he teased.

"I did a film like this, I think," came a deep voice from the gate. Cliff and David walked into the back yard. "'cept there was a pool and a randy pool boy."

"Hi guys!" Sandy gleamed, as she ran and gave the two a hug. "Thank you so much for helping out!"

"No problem," David said. "What do you need us to do?"

"Well, most everything is done until the food arrives," Steve answered. "Are those your costumes?" he asked, pointing to the bags Cliff held.

"Yep. That's them," David smiled. "You're going to love them!"

"Shouldn't you be getting ready?" Cliff inquired.

"Actually, yes," Sandy agreed.

"Do me a favor and get that grill going," Steve said. "We're going to go shower."

Sandy giggled. "We'll be back guys," she assured them. "If the food arrives and we're not outside yet, just start setting it out."

"Will do," David said as the young couple made their way into the house.

"Come on, big guy," David said, squeezing Cliff's massive bicep. "Let's get that grill started, you hot piece of beef."

CHAPTER 4

It was still early in the evening when Melinda stood on her front porch watching the party-goers parading past her house to the Jones'. She was relieved that she had not caved into the itch that pleaded to attend the gathering as well. The costumes were simply outrageous! Some could barely be called costumes at all. Men in togas and loin cloths, women in spiked braziers and cleavage-enhancing gowns. Why, it was nearly Sodom and Gomorrah on Jasper Lane! It was certainly not a party suited to children. If she had seen any children making their way to the party, she might have been tempted to call the police and make an indecency complaint.

It did sound as if the party was fun, though. The music was thumping and the food smelled wonderful, even from where she stood. The desire to join the festivities surged up in her again, but she beat it down with a deep breath.

"I'm fine right here," she whispered. "I'm just fine." She scratched an itch on her elbow impatiently, and then seated herself on the porch swing.

It was nice to have some time alone. Her mother's stay had become a little taxing, her flatulence a little too much to bear. Thankfully, she was inside watching a parade on TV, grumping every now and then at the indecency of some of the float participants. Frank was working another holiday, but that was all right. She knew he was doing it all for her and their wayward son. She chided herself whenever she caught herself thinking her husband was intentionally staying away from home, leaving her with Nanna as if she were a girl again. She was realizing slowly that theirs was a marriage of favors-he got her away from Nanna, she gave him the son she thought he wanted-but still, couldn't he at least pretend to care? Did she know Frank at all?

The screen door opened as someone came out onto the porch. Melinda sighed, thinking it was Nanna coming to destroy her peace. She was surprised, however, when Patrick sat down beside her.

"Hi, Mom," he said, rather timidly. She recognized the tone. It was how he sounded whenever he wanted to do something of which he was afraid she might not approve.

"I'm sorry, Patrick, but the answer is still no. I won't allow you to spend time with those people. I don't want you to be corrupted by their lifestyle." She prepared herself for his anger.

"That's okay," he said. "I don't really care about that anymore."

"Oh?" Melinda looked at him with a motherly mixture of concern and suspicion.

"Yeah," he reiterated. "Maybe you're right. Maybe I shouldn't go over there." She was stunned by his turnabout. "Oh. Okay," she stammered.

"But I don't want to spend any time with the Bible study group either, Mom."

"Patrick, those are good kids. God-fearing kids."

"Maybe," Patrick shrugged. "But they're not my type of kids. And, trust me, they're not as innocent and god-fearing as you think."

She was taken aback by this revelation. Was there some gossip-rather, news-that she should hear about as a concerned parent?

"Mom, do you think kids our age don't know how to manipulate our parents so that we get exactly what we want?"

"Well, I don't know," she replied, staring at a passing menagerie of costumed party people. She paused momentarily. "So, what do you want to do?" she asked. "Who do you want to hang out with?"

"I want a job. I want to make my own money."

"You could mow lawns here in the neighborhood, or work at the church."

Patrick gave her a resentful glare. "No, Mom. I don't want to work there and you know it."

"Then where?"

"Cassie Bloom offered me a job taking care of her pool." He swallowed. It was at this point that his happiness would be decided, at least for the duration of his time living on Jasper Lane. He waited an excruciating minute for her to respond.

"Well," she contemplated. "I don't see why not."

Patrick let out a sigh of relief.

"But you know Cassie is … a different sort of woman. I don't care for many of her vices, but she is a respectable person. Very highly thought of."

"I know," Patrick said. He would have agreed with anything she had said.

"You just need to promise me that if anything immoral happens, you'll quit, right then and there."

"Yes. Yes. I promise," he said, rising to his feet. "Thanks, Mom!" he exclaimed, bending to give her a hug.

She accepted the hug with a surprised smile.

Yes. Cassie's would be a good place for Patrick to work. Melinda would be able to keep her eye on him, and there was the added bonus that it might bring her and Cassie closer together. She could uproot that Becky Ridgeworth from her favored position. Melinda's place in the neighborhood could indeed rise. Cassie giving Patrick a job might be just the thing to put Melinda in the top echelon of neighborhood women, possibly even the town council. Her heart raced at the notion. She would be able to have her own parties, but she would invite only the most proper individuals. Everyone would be so envious! She could turn the street around. No more half naked men would be allowed to go running around. And maybe she could even get a lawn contest started, though that would be unfair because she would always win.

As Melinda's mind sped through these thoughts, Patrick headed back inside the house, happy for the first time in quite a while. As he opened the door, he saw Nanna standing beside the door.

"I'll be watching you," she warned him. "I heard every word, and I'll be watching you."

Patrick's face lost its glow, and he turned from the old woman, making his way upstairs.

Nanna watched after him like a hawk spying a field mouse.

The Jones' Fourth of July party was in full swing. The crowd of extravagantly dressed friends and neighbors danced, ate, and flirted along with the pulse of the music. Steve did his grilling dressed as a younger, sexier Uncle Sam—or Uncle Samson, as he called it. His jacket sleeves had been cut off to reveal his well-defined arms.

Sandy flitted about as a bustier version of Lady Liberty, making sure she greeted everyone. She was having trouble keeping her breasts tucked in the ensemble, but wasn't too terribly concerned about it. Everyone in attendance had most likely already seen her boobs, either by peering over the back fence as she sunbathed nude, or during one of her drunken strip-offs.

She spotted the foursome of David, Cliff, Terrence, and the new guy, Rick (to whom she had just been introduced), by the buffet table.

"How do you think it's going?" she asked, drink in hand.

"It's marvelous!" Terrence cheered. "It looks great!"

"Everyone does seem to be having a good time," she agreed, pride in her voice. She paused to review their costumes.

"I'm Aquaman," Terrence explained, answering her expression.

"The superhero from Saturday mornings?" she asked.

"Yeah," David answered for him. "He heard Hot UPS Guy was coming as Batman, so he wanted to participate in the fetish."

"But, then, shouldn't you be Robin, if he came as Batman?" she inquired.

"Not with this body!" Terrence said. "This is a swimmer's build. Besides, Aquaman is so much hotter."

She giggled at the huge bulge in his green tights, then looked at Rick with a smile that hid slight disappointment at his choice.

"I'm not very good at costumes," the eye-patched cowboy confessed. "I'll do better next time."

"That's okay, honey." She touched his shoulder gently.

"I have to say, though," Terrence confided. "Cliff here has the most eye-popping outfit."

And Sandy agreed with that assessment whole-heartedly. David was nicely attired in a tuxedo and top hat, but it was Cliff who completed the costume: He was the bride to David's groom. A small veil covered his head, which he swept back in order to sip his drink; an extra-extra-large white satin corset was barely keeping his pectorals contained; tiny, white panties hardly disguised his manhood, and did nothing to hide his ass, as his thong-parted rear-end was discreetly covered by a tiny train. He was doing his best to maneuver about in high heels.

"You look so cute!" she exclaimed to them both.

"Thanks," Cliff grumbled, "but these heels are going to have to go … and soon!"

"Oh, baby," David patted him on the arm. "Stop your bitchin'," he admonished, giving the big guy a playful swat on the butt.

"Terrence, there's your Dark Knight," Rick pointed across the yard.

"Yay!" Terrence gleamed. "I'll see y'all later," he said, as he swaggered over in the direction of the Caped Crusader.

"Take off those heels and let's dance … baby," David lustily teased Cliff.

"They're all nuts," Rick said to Sandy, as the bride and groom made their way to the patch of ground designated as the dance floor for the evening.

"We're all a little nuts here," Sandy winked.

Suddenly, the entire party seemed to come to a breathless pause, as everyone's attention was momentarily drawn to the gate. There, standing ostentatiously in regal garb, posed Salome and the Queen of Sheba, otherwise known as Cassie Bloom and Vera.

"Your queens are here!" Cassie declared, her right arm flung up in a dramatic gesture to the sky that would have made Andrew Lloyd Webber proud. Her jewels glittered and danced in the fading sunlight. Vera, too, stood with her chest proud and a look of supremacy on her face. Colored plumes sprouted from various points on her costume.

Becky Ridgeworth, herself dressed as Mrs. Slocombe from the British sitcom *Are You Being Served?*, screeched in delight. "Cassie! How Biblical!"

She ran up to her two friends, embracing them, her large magenta wig getting tangled a bit in the jewelry.

Sandy turned her attention back to Rick. "Oh my," she rolled her eyes affectionately. "Excuse me, Rick," she said, as she walked to the two newest arrivals.

Rick picked up a plate from the table and began perusing the dinner selection.

"Good. I'm starving," came a voice from behind.

James also picked up a plate, and stood next to Rick.

"Hi," Rick said, surprised.

"Hey," James smiled. "Nice outfit," he said.

"Oh," Rick dismissed the compliment. "I guess the more appropriate attire would have been a pirate costume, but everyone would have been expecting that."

"No. I like this," James assured him. "You've got a whole Rooster Cogburn thing going on."

"Who?"

"It's an old movie. Never mind."

"So, where's your costume?"

"I couldn't think of one," James replied. "I'm not very good at that sort of thing." He was dressed in the same khaki shorts and t-shirt Rick had seen him wearing earlier at the grocery store.

"Me neither," Rick confessed. He looked around the party nervously, completely forgetting about the food. Everyone else seemed at ease with one another, jovial and without any nasty inhibitions.

"Do you want to find a less crowded spot?" James asked, perceiving Rick's discomfort.

"Where?"

"This is a big yard. There's got to be somewhere that isn't so packed."

"Sure," Rick agreed, staring into James' eyes. When he realized he was gazing like a crushing kid on a school bus, he bowed his head a little, and covered his eye patch nervously.

James took hold of the hand covering his eye. "Come on," he urged gently.

James and Rick found an abandoned table in the back. The sun had set, and the strung lights glowed around them like lightning bugs suspended in time. They could hear one another better away from the pounding of Steve's music.

"Do you miss it? The military?" Rick asked.

"Sometimes," James responded. "I miss the order. I miss knowing what I was going to be doing and when I was going to be doing it. I'm not so good at organizing my daily routine. There's just so much to do."

"Well, you certainly have your jogs scheduled. Terrence and David set their days by you."

"Yeah," James laughed. "I see them out there."

"You don't mind it?"

"No, not really," he shrugged. "Today was the first I'd seen you out there, though."

"I'm not much for gawking," Rick said, slightly embarrassed.

"I'm glad you were out there."

Rick let out a nervous laugh, then looked to the table, playing with a napkin, as his hand instinctively shielded his eye patch.

"Why do you do that?" James asked.

"Do what?"

"Cover your eye like that?"

"I'm self-conscious about it, I suppose."

"You shouldn't be," James said, again taking Rick's hand down. "Look at me, Rick," he said.

Rick raised his chin, and looked into James' eyes.

"It's a battle scar," James posited. "That's all. We all have them." He pulled down his shorts a tiny bit. Rick was a little startled by the suddenness of the action. What was he doing? Was he asking for a blow-job? In the Jones' back yard?

Then he saw the deep, thick gash of a scar on James' hip.

"Did you get that in the military?"

"Yep. Shrapnel. Cut a huge gash in my thigh. Hurt like hell." He pulled his shorts back up.

"But that's different," Rick said. "That was in battle. What happened to me was … just silly in comparison."

"Rick, personal battles should never be compared. Your battles are every bit as hard as mine in their own way."

Rick stared at him, silent for a moment. "Thanks," he whispered.

James smiled and squeezed his hand on the table.

"I have another," Rick offered.

"Oh, yeah?"

"I had brain surgery when I was a young kid. Cavernous himangiomas." He laughed at a memory. "When I woke up in the hospital afterward, my brother asked if the surgery had made me straight."

"Family … What are you gonna do with them, huh?"

The moment was interrupted by a loud bellow from the house.

"What is *that*?" James inquired, glancing to the house. "I'll get my gun and we can put it out of its misery."

Closer to the house, Steve had set up the karaoke machine, and Becky Ridgeworth was doing her best rendition of Mrs. Slocombe singing "I Will Survive." She was clearly intoxicated, standing on of the buffet table in the platter with the pigs-in-blankets. Cassie and Vera cheered her on, climbing on the table themselves after the first stanza.

"And this is where I chose to move," James said sarcastically.

Rick laughed. "It's not so bad. At least, it's not boring here."

"I'm never going to have a solid routine again, I'm afraid," James joked, drawing a finger along Rick's knuckles as their hands rested together on the table.

As most of the revelers carried on out of doors, Terrence had succeeded in very quickly convincing Hot UPS Guy to sneak into the house through the sliding doors. He led him by the hand down the hallway to Steve's office in back.

"Are you sure about this?" the costumed packager asked.

"We're all good friends," Terrence assured him. "Don't worry about it."

Once in the room, Terrence wasted no time. He tore at the bat costume like a man consumed, his teeth biting the newly exposed nipple. Hot UPS Guy reciprocated by kissing him roughly on the lips. Terrence felt himself burning, his blood boiling, as the Caped Crusader's hands groped and squeezed his ass, ripping a hole in his green tights. The thumping bass outside only added to the savage feel of the moment, his superhero fetish finally come to life.

Hot UPS Guy moaned as Terrence licked his way down his stomach.

"Yes! Yes! Suck it!" he whispered, as Terrence nearly tore off the stubborn utility belt, and pulled the hard, Prince Albert-adorned cock from the Bat thong.

"Fuck, yeah!" he groaned in delight, as Terrence swallowed it.

Becky nearly fell off the table a couple of times before the end of her exuberant performance. She got through it safely, though, and was helped down. Cassie and Vera stayed atop the buffet, however, and began a very combative and dramatic version of "Does He Love You?"

David and Cliff watched with the bemused crowd.

"Good stuff," Cliff snickered.

"Sure is."

"My ass is a little sore. People keep smacking it." The big guy rubbed his back end with playful unease.

David turned around for a quick crowd scan. Steve was stepping out the side gate. It wasn't a sneaky move; it was more like that of a man with something more important on his mind.

"I'll be back," David told his bride and headed for the gate.

Steve was sitting on the curb when David came upon him.

"Mind if I have a seat?" he asked, his top hat in his hands. It had given him an extreme case of hat hair.

"Be my guest," Steve answered, glancing up to his friend. He hugged his knees and sighed as if there were something he just couldn't figure out.

"So, what's up?" David asked. "What's eating you?"

"Is it that obvious?"

"Well, it's not subtle, my friend. Anyone who knows you well can see that there's something going on. Now spill it."

"It's just me and Sandy ..."

"Are there problems?"

"Nothing like you think," Steve assured him. "We're still in love. Everything's still fine. But, therein lays the problem. I love her so much. I hate disappointing her like this." His eyes were watering, his voice cracking.

"How would you be disappointing her, Steve? You're a great husband."

"Thanks," Steve said, somewhat dispassionately. "I lost my job, David. They fired me. The firm folded."

"Jesus, Steve, I'm sorry."

The raucous party went on behind them, oblivious to the delicate moment.

"Sandy wanted to go on with the party. She loves the Fourth. But, Dave, I don't know what we're going to do. How are we going to get by after our savings run out? It's hard finding any kind of job out there."

"There's nothing in your field?"

"Not that I can find."

David paused, coming upon an idea. "Have you given thought to other careers?"

"What could I do?" Steve asked. "What could I do?" he repeated, quietly, and more to himself. "Do you know of something?" he asked, looking pleadingly to his friend.

"Never mind," David said. "It was a crazy idea."

"No. David, tell me. Please. I'll try anything." His eyes were begging for some type of resolution, some answer.

"Well," David replied, after a pause, "there's this new company that Cliff knows about. They need guys ... actors."

"What kind of actors?" Steve asked a little suspiciously.

"The kind you're thinking of," David confirmed. "It's basically a gay-for-pay operation. These straight guys come in, get it off with another straight guy, pick up a nice paycheck, and then they're done. Takes about a day. If you're a hit, you can make a nice bit of cash off the DVD sales and the internet sites."

Steve stared at him, unblinking.

"See," David said. "It's a bad idea. Forget I said anything."

"How much cash?" Steve asked, before his better judgment kicked in. "Never mind!" he exclaimed. "Don't tell me. I don't want to know."

"It's not your thing anyway."

"No. God, no!" Steve laughed. "Shit! What am I going to do, David?"

A sudden burst of laughter from the revelers brought their attention back to the house.

"What do you suppose is going on in there?" Steve asked, staring over his shoulder.

"Well, no one's singing, so that's a plus."

Sandy came bursting out of the gate, laughing uncontrollably.

"David," she choked out, "Terrence ..." She pointed to the house. "You have got to see this! He needs your ... assistance."

David and Steve glanced at one another in bewilderment before racing back to the party.

They made their way into the house, through the throng of costumed guests who lined the halls, all of them giggling and drunk.

"Aaargh! Don't move!" came a shout from Steve's office.

"What the hell?" David gasped, as he came upon the scene.

"Isn't it too much?" Cassie Bloom guffawed, slapping David on the shoulder.

In front of them, in much anguish and fear, stood Hot UPS Guy, nearly de-costumed, with Aqua-man, aka Terrence, attached to his groin area.

"What happened here?" David inquired, a smile creeping onto his astonished face.

"Terrence's tongue ring," Cassie explained between bursts of laughter, "it got caught on Batman's Prince Albert and ... bat thong!"

The crowd erupted into roars.

"I'm sorry, Terrence," Sandy said. "We're not laughing at you. It's just the situation."

"Somebody do something!" Hot UPS Guy screamed, clearly not amused.

"David!" Terrence tried to say.

"Don't say anything!" UPS Guy yelled at him.

David approached and inspected the situation.

"We can do this easily," he assured the two tangled superheroes. "But first, I'm unfortunately going to have to do something you might not appreciate."

Terrence eyed him suspiciously from the side.

David whipped out a digital era from his tux pocket. "Sorry," he said. "This'll make a great Christmas card."

Click!

Terrence made a frantic grab for the camera, which caused him to pull on UPS Guy, which, in turn, caused him to scream in agony.

David gave the camera to Steve to hold.

"Now," David said. "Let's get that dick out of your mouth."

Patrick watched from his driveway as the party let out. It was easier to sneak out at night. His parents were asleep, being "decent" folk who got to bed at appropriate hours. Nanna was his only major hurdle. She would, at times, stay up all night watching old black-and-white movies in the living room. To avoid her, Patrick would steal through the back door. In reality, however, it wouldn't have mattered if Nanna ever told Melinda of Patrick's night-time sojourns outside. His mother would find him simply lounging on a chair, counting the stars, or waiting for the first streaks of dawn in the sky. It would just be another of his habits that would strike her as bizarre.

The goings-on at the Jones residence, though, had Patrick forgoing the star-gazing experience in the back, and focusing instead on the glittering stars passing on the pavement in front of him. Fireworks could still be seen in the distance from other people's parties.

After a while, he saw Cassie Bloom emerge from the festivities. He realized that the soiree was very nearly over. Without Cassie, he knew, there was no party. With her came Vera and Becky. Becky said goodnight and departed for her home.

Cassie and Vera began walking to the cul de sac when Cassie spotted Patrick sitting on the drive.

"I'll be home in a minute," she said to Vera as she walked over to the Gold residence.

Vera waved to Patrick and continued on her way home, singing "Summertime" as she went.

"You're up late," Cassie observed, pulling her gold shawl around her. Her jewelry jingled. A slight chill was in the air.

"So are you," Patrick countered.

"Well, it was a late party, and I do love a party."

"From what I've heard, it wouldn't be a party without you." He rose to his feet, wrapping his arms around his shoulders.

"Oh?"

"Yeah. You being the grand dame of Jasper Lane and all."

She laughed at his description of her. "Do you wish you had been at the party tonight, Patrick?"

He shrugged. "I don't know. Maybe, though I don't really know anyone."

"Well, that will change when you start working for me," she assured him.

"I don't think Mom will approve."

"Of course not," Cassie gleamed with a wicked grin and a wink.

He returned her smile.

"Patrick," she said, placing her hand on his arm, "you're going to have fun working for me. I promise. We'll find you some joy. We'll get wind to fill your sails, I swear it."

CHAPTER 5

Patrick found working for Cassie as freeing as he hoped it would be. He was shown the ropes for the first few days, and by the end of the week, he was working on his own as Cassie sunned herself. Near lunch time, Cassie would head into the house and return to the pool with food and refreshments. Though she was easily in her mid-fifties, Cassie had taken good care of her outward appearance. She could still turn heads.

Patrick felt at ease, as if a strangling weight was lifted from him for at least a few hours each day. He was usually done with the work before lunch, but Cassie would find him something else to do. She could tell from his expression that he wanted to stay away from his own home for as long as possible. And the truth was she enjoyed having him around.

"Is Nanna still causing you problems?" Cassie asked one afternoon near the end of his first work week. They sat at a glass table, under a large, white umbrella. Cassie worked at peeling an orange with her long fingernails. She wore playfully large sunglasses, and her hair was covered by a blue bandanna which matched her bathing suit.

"Yeah," Patrick replied, wolfing down the cheeseburger she had made for him. "She watches me every morning when I leave. It's creepy, but she's always been a freaky old bitch."

"Patrick, how did you come from them?" Cassie inquired. "You're such good stock."

"I dunno," Patrick shrugged. "Just lucky, I guess. Thems the breaks, you know?"

Cassie laughed. "You remind me of my son, Jason. You've got the same dry … desperation."

"Does it come off as despair?"

"Probably not to most, but I can tell." Cassie paused in reflection. "I know it all too well."

"But you've got such a great place, and everyone loves you. How could you be despairing about anything?" He was genuinely incredulous.

"I've got money, yes. And things. Lots and lots of pointless things." She leaned back in her chair, gesturing around her with a fluid sweep. "But it isn't worth anything without someone here to share it with me."

"Why don't you call your son?"

"It's not that easy, sweetie," Cassie said with melancholy in her voice. "Sometimes the hardest thing to do is forgive someone. Most times the truth does more harm than good."

"I don't believe you did it," Patrick offered. "I don't think you killed him … your husband, I mean. How does anyone know if he's even dead, you know?"

Cassie smiled. "Thank you, darling," she said.

She watched as he continued eating, stuffing the burger into his mouth as if he hadn't eaten in weeks. If only it *were* that simple. If only Jason believed her lie, or knew the man his father really was. If he only knew what his father was going to do to him. But there were no easy ways to explain things, and that's what the real problem was. Unlike Cassie, most of the world saw things as black and white, right and wrong. She knew, however, that there were, and had always been, only a million shades of in between. Truth was paper-thin, and one could easily fall right through it.

"Haven't seen you use the pool yet," Cassie said, interrupting her own thoughts.

"I'm not a big swimmer," Patrick replied. "I don't even swim in my own pool."

"Do you know how?"

"Yeah. Just don't care for it." He finished his meal, licking his fingers of the mustard and salt, then took a breathless gulp of his iced tea.

"Well, if you change your mind, I bought you a pair of swimming trunks. They're in the changing room."

"Thanks!" He suddenly recognized some matronly need on her face. "Maybe I will swim later," he said to appease her. "I mean, your pool *is* bigger, after all."

She nodded and sighed. "Good. Besides, I'm going to want everyone to be having fun when I have guests over for a cocktail. That includes my employees."

The corner of his mouth lifted like a lopsided window shade.

Outside the pool area, doing her best to peer through the bushes and fence, Nanna kept an eye on her grandson. She had nothing better to do with her time than spend the afternoon spying on Patrick. If he did anything that was immoral, anything that Melinda would not, or should not, approve of, she would know.

"Little brat!" she whispered.

But her location was nearly given away. A loud, untamable burst of gas escaped from her, scaring a crow that had perched on a nearby tree. She almost fell trying to get out of the bushes and make her way back home.

Iron & Wine played gently on the stereo as Rick read David's article in *Gay Men's Fitness* on the seven best exercises for "Blasting That Booty." It wasn't his usual reading material, but he couldn't find any good books lying around, no Faulkner or James Purdy, and all Terrence had were *Vogue* and *Midwest Living*. Besides, it was easy reading which was vital with the eye patch still taking some getting used to, and the photographs were undeniably fun to look at. Still, cheesy jokes about "one-eyed monsters" plagued him.

Rick was distracted from his reading as Terrence moped into the room and fell backward on the bed in faux exhaustion. He breathed out an attention-seeking sigh.

"Problems, Terrence?" Rick asked, putting the magazine down on the bed beside him.

"What is this depressing music?" Terrence remarked.

"It's good music. You know, the type with lyrics, the type you can actually make sense of."

"Well, you can't dance to it."

"No. I suppose not. But then, I never was much of a dancer. That was you." Rick paused. "So, what's up?"

"I just got off the phone with Christian," Terrence explained, his eyes on the high ceiling. "He wanted to know why I wasn't married. He wanted to know if he had any brothers or sisters."

"And what did you tell him in that big butch voice of yours."

"I told him I hadn't found the right ... person."

"Ah," Rick nodded in understanding. "The pronoun game."

"I don't know. I think he's getting close to the truth."

"So? That's a good thing, Terrence. You have got to be honest with him. You're making it sound like a Tom Clancy thriller. *Don't let him get too close! Then we'll have to kill him.*"

"I know. I will. But it's too soon. I'm afraid if I tell him now, it'll scare him away."

"That's sweet."

"What?" Terrence inquired, looking to Rick.

"You're warming to the idea of being a father."

Terrence didn't respond. He simply stared at Rick, almost through him, contemplating what he had just said.

"My carefree days are over," he finally moaned.

"Oh," Rick groaned, kicking him lightly. "Stop being so morbid. He's a grown boy. You don't need to raise him. You can go on living just as randomly as you ever did."

"Cross your fingers for me."

"Terrence, stop with the self-pity. You're still as promiscuous as ever. Guys aren't going to look at you any differently."

"I'm used goods," Terrence cried, upping the dramatics. "I've sired offspring!"

"Oh, good lord!" Rick remarked, exasperated. "Here!" He threw his cell phone at Terrence. "Call Hot UPS Guy. Go get your rocks off."

"Get my rocks off?" Terrence mocked. "Who says that? Besides, I can't. We're no longer seeing each other."

"Because of the incident at the party?"

"The *incident*?" Mocking again. "I didn't just spill fruit juice on his shorts, Ricky. I almost tore the poor guy's dick off."

"Yeah. That's true. I've got no compassion for you there."

"He said he didn't want to get into anything with me. He thinks I'm too rough. Ha! Too rough? He was the one digging into my ass like he was peeling an orange."

"Well, go out to a club then. Get your mind off fatherhood for the night."

"Maybe you're right," Terrence responded. "Wanna come along?"

"Nope. I've already got a date tonight, thank you."

"That's right," Terrence said, leaning on his elbow. "You're dating Mr. Army Man. Date number two, right?"

"Correct." Even when Rick was excited, it sounded as if he was about to kill himself.

"Lucky asshole."

"Yeah, I'm lucky. Rick the One-Eyed is lucky! Cyclops is lucky!"

"Now who's being over-dramatic?" Terrence teased.

Rick picked up the magazine and threw it.

Steve couldn't focus. Every day gone without finding a job meant one more day dipping into their savings. He had gotten some bites, even an interview with a large firm, but that was two weeks away. And even if he did get that job, it would be like Sandy said. He would most likely never make the same level of pay that he previously had. His stomach ached with worry.

He sat on the stoop of the porch, lacing up his running shoes. A good jog just might clear his head for a bit.

"Going for a run, baby?" Sandy asked, stepping out onto the porch languidly.

"Yeah. I just need to get the heart pumping, you know? Haven't been able to get any cardio in for the last few days."

"Steven Emory Jones, you're not making yourself sick with worry, are you?"

"No," he lied. "No. Of course not. We'll figure it out." He stood and kissed her on the cheek. "Be back soon," he said, taking off with a gentle stride.

"We'll figure it out," Sandy whispered as she watched him go.

Steve ran for a while, thinking about possible solutions, jobs he could apply for. He would even consider moving if the pay was right. They loved the neighborhood, but it looked as if they were not going to be able to make ends meet unless something fantastic came along soon. Maybe they should start playing the lottery.

His head spun with negative thoughts, impossibilities. His aggravation only spurred him on until he was heading back to Jasper Lane, having at last nearly circled the entire neighborhood. He slowed and checked his racing heart rate. He stood with his hands on his hips, and closed his eyes. Not only were his lungs about to explode, but his stomach was still a mess and his head had begun to hurt.

A slight breeze cooled him off, blowing over his sweat-soaked tank top.

"Steve, are you okay?"

Steve opened his eyes to see David and Cliff, both shirtless and glistening, walking toward him.

"Yeah," Steve said. He wiped his forehead with his arm. "Just wanted to get out and think about things for a while. I'm good." He felt dizzy, almost faint. It reminded him of the time he had over-exerted himself training in college.

"Looks like you pushed yourself pretty hard," Cliff noticed.

Steve nodded. "Maybe a little too hard. You two gettin' her done, too, huh?"

"Yeah," David said. "Cliff here isn't much of a runner, though."

"I've got too much muscle. It takes a lot of effort," Cliff defended.

"But at least we look good, right?" David winked. "Gives us a good tan anyway."

"We'll run home with you, Steve," Cliff offered.

"Cool," Steve remarked, as the three jogged slowly down Jasper Lane. He couldn't help but be awed by Cliff's massive pectorals as they jumped and twitched and bounced with every struggling step.

"Jeez, Cliff," he joked. "We're going to need to get you a bra or something."

"Hey!" Cliff yelled, pushing him jovially.

"Steve, keep what I said the other night in mind, okay?" David said.

"David, I can't."

"Just keep it in mind. It's easy money."

"And a lot of it," Cliff interjected.

"Just in case, Steve. I'm worried about you. You look like you're about to have a breakdown."

"I'll keep it in mind," Steve appeased him.

"Promise?"

"I promise, okay?" Steve said. "I appreciate you thinking about us, guys. I mean it. You're good friends."

An awkward, tender moment passed between them. No words were needed or desired.

"There's Melinda Gold," David said, changing the subject.

Melinda stood expectantly at the end of her drive. She stared at them as they approached, clearly wanting to say something.

"Do it!" David encouraged Cliff.

"What's he going to do?" Steve asked.

"Watch."

Cliff leaped at the chance to act upon his comic sensibilities. Steve and David slowed down, and Cliff began running in long, wide strides, simulating slow-motion. He waved at Melinda with a cheesy grin as he ran past her, his chest bouncing obscenely.

Her mouth dropped to the ground.

Steve and David had to stop running. They doubled over laughing and ended up walking the rest of the way.

Rick sat at the candle lit table surrounded by a cozy shade of dark. He was in a carefully decorated dining room. Antiques made up almost every item of furniture, as was the case throughout the house. He noticed the grandeur of it all on the first date the previous week, which was also a quiet dinner at James' home.

"So your uncle left you all his furniture as well?" Rick asked over the pasta Alfredo. "This would be Disneyland for Terrence."

"Yeah," James responded. "The house and everything in it. It's been a bit much for me to take in. I'm still finding things tucked away in closets. Disturbing things." He arched an eyebrow.

"He must have been a character."

"I'm guessing. I don't really know." He paused. "It seems he knew me better than I knew myself, though. I'll have to ask Cassie about him some day. I'm piecing him together from the things I find."

"She would know. She makes everything that goes on around here her business, it seems."

"True," James agreed. "Do you not like the pasta?" he asked, gesturing with his fork to Rick's plate. "You're not eating much."

"No. It's good," Rick assured him, taking a drink of the Zinfandel. "It's just ..."

"What?" He glanced at Rick with penetrating blue eyes. Rick thought he might melt as the flickering light from the candles cast shadows over his face. Eva Cassidy sang "Field of Dreams" behind them.

"Don't get me wrong. I love this. I love the dinner, the candle light, the mood."

"But? Come on, Rick. Be honest with me."

"Why don't we go out some time?" Rick asked. "To a movie or dinner in public. Do you think we can do that? That is, if you're still interested in seeing me." He bowed his head and twisted some pasta onto his fork.

James was silent, and it scared Rick. *This is it,* he thought. *I've blown it. I should have just kept my mouth shut and been happy with this!*

"I would love to," James finally spoke. "Believe me. Really, I would. But ... I'm not completely out, Rick. Not to my friends or family. None of them."

"Why not? I'm not attacking. I just don't understand."

"When I was young, the entire family disowned Uncle Willie. I never understood why. Nobody so much as talked with him. No Christmas cards. Nothing. When he left me this house, I started reading through some old journals and unsent cards he had stockpiled. My uncle was gay, and my mother didn't want anything to do with him. He was my family and nobody even acknowledged his existence."

Rick was listening to every word, understanding peculiar similarities in their perspective circumstances.

"I managed to come see him a couple of times as I got older, but they weren't very long visits. Just five or ten minutes each time. I never understood why he had been cut off. He wouldn't even explain it to me when I asked. He'd shrug and smile."

"So, you think your family would react that way again? To you?"

"I know they would," James replied solidly. "They're stagnant in their perceptions of right and wrong. There's no room for growth there." He took a sip of his wine.

"They're religious, huh?"

"No. That's the weird thing. They've got nothing to base their prejudice on."

"I don't suppose being in the military made being gay any easier, either."

"Not really," James admitted. "But there are ways to meet other guys. There are networks."

"Oh?" Rick raised *his* eyebrow.

James laughed. "Don't worry," he said. "I didn't play around too much. I'm a pretty picky guy."

"I guess, then, I should take that as a compliment."

"Rick," James said, putting his fork down and leaning slightly forward. "You're the best thing I think I might have ever come across."

Rick swallowed. Goosebumps ran across his skin. He reached for his wine, still staring at James.

The music shuffled to Laura Nyro. James rose to his feet and walked over to Rick.

"Let's dance," he said, holding out his hand.

Rick rose and they swayed to Laura's sweet, sad voice. He closed his eyes, feeling their heartbeats locking into one another, smelling James' scent, feeling protected and safe.

"I can play this song for you later," James whispered.

"You're a musician? What instrument?"

"Guitar. I'm not great, but ..."

"I would like that," Rick said. "That would be great." He rested his head on James' shoulder.

David lay on Cliff's chest on the sofa, watching movies in the dark. They were naked but for running shorts. Terrence, in his matching blue pajama set, sat in the arm chair, a bowl of low-fat popcorn keeping him company. Mankewiecz's *Suddenly Last Summer* spear-headed the late-night campfest.

"I love Katharine Hepburn!" he exclaimed. "I have yet to see Our Lady Katie in anything where she wasn't the best thing in it."

"I wish I *was* Kate Hepburn," David said.

"No," Cliff objected, kissing him gently on the bare shoulder. "I like you the way you are."

"Oh, puke!" Terrence cried, throwing unpopped kernels at them.

"You're not drinking tonight," David observed. "What's the matter, pumpkin? Finally shit your liver out?"

"Very funny," Terrence replied. "I just, uh, don't feel like drinking is all."

"*You* don't feel like drinking?" Cliff posed.

"Yes! Things are different. I don't know. Since Christian and I have been talking …"

"Aw, that's sweet!" David chuckled.

"Shut up!" Terrence chirped. "Watch the damn movie!"

"Oh! Liz Taylor's flashback!" David said. "I love this scene."

Deliciously, Elizabeth Taylor screamed in overripe abundance as Sebastian was eaten alive by angry, starving children. The cordless phone inappropriately rang somewhere beneath the cushions of the sofa. Cliff fumbled for it and gave it to David.

"Hello," David answered, after an exasperated groan.

"Hey Dave. It's Steve." He sounded anxious, knocked off-center.

"What's going on, Steve?" David asked, untangling himself from Cliff and rising from his position.

"Sorry to call so late, but …"

"Steve? What is it?" He walked into the kitchen and sat at the island.

"Sandy's pregnant," Steve said.

"That's great!" David exclaimed. "Congratulations!" He paused, remembering Steve and Sandy's money issues. "It *is* great, right?"

The question caught Steve off-guard. "Yeah … yes, absolutely! It's great! We're excited."

"But scared," David finished the thought for him.

"Scared as hell, David."

"We'll be here for you. You know that."

"I know," Steve replied. "That's why I called, actually."

There was a long halt in conversation as Sandy came into the room. David heard them discussing who was on the phone, heard Sandy pitch a cheery 'hello' his way across the line. When she left, Steve resumed the conversation.

"Dave, I need a favor."

"Anything," David promised.

"Could you … could you get Cliff to check into that gay-for-pay idea for me?"

"Are you sure, Steve?"

"No," he said, breathlessly, then, "Yes. I think I'm sure. We need the money, Dave. I'm desperate. But Sandy just can't find out. *She can't.*"

"I understand," David said. He suddenly felt like the hit man in a mob movie. "It'll be okay, Steve."

"Yeah," Steve tried reassuring himself. "It'll all work out."

CHAPTER 6

"This was a fantastic idea," James complimented Rick as they walked among parents and their children. "A day trip to the zoo. I haven't been to a zoo since I was a kid."

"Yeah, but now you don't have to worry about getting yelled at when you wander off."

"Are you planning to lose me?" James joked.

They stopped at the meerkat exhibit. The skinny little creatures scampered about with quick, shooting movements, as children giggled all around. It was a lovely morning for it. And it wasn't very crowded either. Of course, this wasn't the only zoo in the area, but it was by far the smallest. James and Rick leaned over the railing. James sipped at a cola, while Rick pecked at a bag of chips. He still got the odd stare from small children who didn't know any better than to point at the eye patch, but it was becoming less of an issue with James beside him.

"Cute little rats, huh?" Rick said.

"Busy as all get out. What do you think is going through their heads?"

"Where am I? Where am I?" Rick responded in a high voice.

"What are they doing?" James cocked his head, watching the randy meerkats.

"I think they're going for meerkittens."

"Eeew, Mommy!" cried a little girl nearby as she pointed and jumped up and down.

"Where are the big cats?" James asked. "I want to see big cats."

"You're a big cat," Rick kidded, as they walked away from the mating furries.

"What's that mean?" James laughed.

"I don't know," Rick smiled and bumped into James playfully.

"Ah! The King!" James proclaimed as they came upon the lions. The largest one, a male, sat near a lioness.

"Look at that," Rick said. "Majestic."

Suddenly, the lion pounced upon the lioness, rutting and growling.

James and Rick laughed and began to walk away.

"Must be something in the air," said James.

"You think?" Rick glanced at him with a flirtatious eye.

"I know. I feel it too. I smell it. It smells like ... like ... like you."

Rick stared at him, both with caution and desire. He swallowed hard and focused on the zebras ahead.

"I enjoy our time together," Rick admitted as he blushed. "I haven't had fun in so long ..."

"That's a shame, Rick. You deserve it. You should have all the fun you want. Would you let me be the one to give it to you?"

"Give what?" Rick winked.

James grinned. "Now, there you go. Ruining a perfectly good heartfelt moment with depraved sexual innuendo."

"You don't want my sexual innuendo?"

"Show me yours, I'll show you mine." He saw a shocked look sweep across Rick's face. "I'm sorry. That was a really bad line. I shouldn't have ..."

"No. It wasn't you. Look at that!"

Rick pointed to the zebras, two males. It was very apparent they were male because their long erect penises wagged back and forth as they stared at one another.

"I wonder if that's a challenge or an entreaty," James spoke.

Rick shrugged. "Show me yours, I'll show you mine."

"What do you think?" Steve inquired, as he studied himself in the gym mirror wall. The gym was fairly empty around lunchtime. Only a few careless clangs from dumbbells and racks could be heard.

"About what?" David asked.

Steve still studied himself. He flexed his triceps and biceps, then raised his shirt to inspect his abdominal region. "Do you think I'll be any good? Do you think the gay guys will like me?"

"Steve, you're a hot guy. They're going to love you. You look great."

"Yeah. It's a good thing I know my way around the gym."

"Unlike some." David nodded in the direction of the cardiovascular equip-ment. Terrence, who had asked to tag along as part of his new more adult per-sona, was struggling with an elliptical. So unfamiliar was he with the proper use of the machine, he nearly did the splits.

"The things we do for acceptance, huh?" Steve grinned. "I'm sure the kid will love him no matter what."

"We've told him. He won't listen. He's certain he has to become this Ward Cleaver or Dick van Dyke."

David found a bench and began doing crunches.

"So, how are you feeling about all this?" he asked in between breaths. "About being in a porn?"

"I'm not sure. I mean, I know it's not what I'd want to do if I had a choice, but … it seems my choices have all run out on me. And Sandy … she expects a certain lifestyle. You remember how well-off her folks are."

David rose to his feet. "Steve, I'm sure she would understand. It's hard out there. Jobs are slim. Perhaps she could get a job."

"No," Steve said defiantly. "No. I'm the provider. I'm the caretaker. I like it that way. There is something to be said for old-fashioned thinking."

David smiled. "I guess."

Terrence had moved on to the stair climber. He was having difficulty with the pedals, as well as the monitor.

"I'll be back. Terry's getting frustrated."

"Fucker!" David heard Terrence curse the machine as he approached.

"Problems?"

"I can't figure this out! It won't work. It's broken." He stopped stepping for a moment. "Hey!" he shouted at the front desk. "Your machine's broken!"

"Terrence!" David hushed him. He waved off the help from the gym attendee. "Jesus! I can't take you anywhere."

"It's broken, David!" Terrence snapped.

"It is not. Look." A few seconds later the monitor was alight with bright red numbers.

"How'd you program in my weight? You don't know how much I weigh."

"I guessed. Just climb. I'm going back to the dumbbells."

As David walked away, he heard a shrill shriek. He turned to see Terrence staring at the monitor with his mouth agape.

"These machines are awful!" Terrence cried.

David approached and saw what had distressed him so. Someone had figured out how to key in sentences for the scroll across the top. Where it usually read *Keep it up! You're doing great!*, it now said *Faster, you fat ass!*

Melinda walked down Jasper Lane, toward James Tucker's house, gently holding the sealed, scented, pretty blue envelope in hand. At last, after many drafts, she had written a note that was both gracious and firm. She could not tolerate his flagrant half-naked strutting any longer, and she had finally found the words to tell him so. Melinda was proud of her command of vocabulary. Mr. Tucker would surely understand. She hummed "Summertime" as she neared the mailbox.

Suddenly, Gayhound darted out in front of her, chasing a bee. Melinda tripped, trying to avoid falling on the animal, and instead fell onto the lawn beside the walkway. The letter had fallen from her grasp and lay a few feet away on the grass. The slight breeze was brushing it gently along the close-cut blades. Too closely cut, Melinda thought.

Gayhound returned and found the movement of the letter to be of some interest.

"Gayhound!" Melinda admonished, cringing as she said the foul name. "No! Stay away from that!"

She leaped to her high heels, but was too late. Gayhound sniffed at the blue envelope, looked back at Melinda, then lifted his leg and marked his territory.

"Shoo!"

Gayhound barked at her and quickly bounded away.

Melinda's shoulders hung in hopelessness. All her work was destroyed. Still, she couldn't just leave it lying there. That would be littering.

She snatched up an empty trash bag that was tumble-weeding across the road, and used it as a glove. Carefully, the urine-soaked letter was wrapped in the bag. She would have to do it all over again. But how could she remember her perfectly constructed sentences?

"Fiddle-sticks!" she huffed as she made her way home.

Dusk was settling over the street like satin, cool and refreshing. Patrick sat in the lounge chair by the pool, drinking a bottled cola and chewing on some leftovers Cassie had in the refrigerator. He liked being able to stay away from home, away from the evil eye of Nanna, the scolding tongue of his mother, and the indifference of his father. The best part was Melinda was perfectly fine that he stayed later. Her hunger for social clout in the neighborhood was insatiable.

Cassie had left earlier, headed to Vera's club with Becky and David. Patrick had the house to himself, but all he wanted to do was relax with the quiet evening air. The pool water danced a reflective tango with the pool lights.

Patrick studied the potted plant next to him, giant elephant ears in a concrete vase. He was strumming a finger along a stem of the plant when he noticed a white gleam poking up from the rich soil. He dug in, pulling out a long, thin bone. Some small animal or bird, he supposed. It was no larger than a finger.

"We worry so much about how we are seen, and, in the end, this is all that's left. Payment for our hubris."

He stuck the bone back in the soil, wondering what had come over him.

"Hubris? Where the hell did that come from?"

The music pulsed and pounded as bodies flailed in chaotic unison on the dance floor, saturated by dazzling colors. Young shirtless men rubbed and gyrated against one another in a ritual known by the proud and lucky few.

"Look at him go!" David cried above the music, sitting at the VIP table overlooking the dance floor at *Vera's*. Cliff was in the center of the frenzied pack, and the boys were worshiping his shirtless, muscular form.

"They love him," Vera responded. "He's a megastar here, baby!"

"He loves it," David grinned. He turned his attention back to his three friends at the table.

"There are some new cuties here tonight, Vera," Cassie observed.

"Fresh meat," interjected an inebriated Becky.

"Not for you, baby. These boys don't want none of your cooter," Vera joked. Becky laughed and gave her a playful jab.

David took on a more serious air as he spoke to Cassie. "Is everything still under the radar? Are we still in the clear?"

"I think so," Cassie answered. "I don't know anyone who would have reason to suspect. Those he worked for were looking to get rid of him somehow, anyway. I'm sure they don't want to raise a stink."

"He left. That's all anyone needs to know," David said. "We should be fine. We just have to give it time."

"Honey," Vera said. "You and Becky don't need to worry about a thing. It wasn't your problem to begin with. You'll never know trouble by Cassie or me."

"Hell with that!" Becky chirped in. "One for all and all for one, right? We're family, no matter what."

"That's right," David agreed, taking hold of Becky's and Cassie's hands.

Vera took hold of Cassie and Becky, forming a circle of strength.

"Isn't there a statute of limitations on things like this?" Becky asked.

"Not on murder, sweetie," David answered.

Cassie tightened her grip on her friends' hands. "Thank you, my friends," she said. "My good friends."

"Come on, honey. I want it. I want it bad. I've been a naughty little girl." Sandy's hand reached down her husband's thigh. It was nearing midnight and Steve had been fighting off her advances for over an hour.

"I can't, Sandy," he moaned. "We've got to think of the baby."

"You're not going to hurt the baby," she assured him. "I can tell you want it." She gripped his penis tightly. His breath was shallow.

"You're sure it won't hurt the baby? The doctor told you this?"

"Everyone knows you can still have fun during pregnancy."

"Really?"

"Baby, the longer you resist, the more turned on I get," she snarled, as she nibbled on his shoulder.

He thought for a moment as he stared into her lusting eyes. She still caressed his manhood.

"Just a minute!" he said suddenly, leaping up from the bed. "I'll be right back!"

"Steve? What is it?" Sandy asked, as Steve ran down the stairs.

In a few minutes he was back in the room, carrying their camcorder and tripod.

Sandy giggled. "What are you doing?"

"Remember when we did this in college? Remember how much fun it was?" He hurriedly set up the equipment.

"Yes," she answered. "And I also remember the football team getting hold of it, and the tape then mysteriously disappearing, never to be seen again."

"That won't happen this time," he promised, getting more aroused by the minute.

"How do you know?"

"No football team."

He leaped on the bed, now completely involved in the adventure.

"What's gotten into you?" she laughed. "Why do you want this taped?"

"I don't know," he grinned. "Could be fun."

CHAPTER 7

Steve was thankful to Cliff and David, though, his fear still clung to him like wet clothes. Cliff had managed to get him a personal interview with a prominent porn producer. He didn't even need to send any preview tape showing his masculine ass in all its glory. He breathed a sigh of relief at that. He realized, though, he would be doing much more than simply shedding his clothes if everything worked out right.

The morning of the great event, Steve washed himself thoroughly. It was the most cleansing shower he could ever remember taking.

The producer, Gabriel, was an amiable guy. He wasn't much older than Steve, and looked respectable, like a lawyer or regular businessman. He was clean-shaven and his office was neat and well-furnished. It wasn't at all what Steve had expected. The stereotype of the porn business had him imagining sticky leather couches and a room that smelled of musk.

As he sat on the plush chair in the producer's office, he found himself becoming more at ease as the conversation hit everything from stocks to politics to books. Steve found that he liked the guy. They could have been fraternity brothers or teammates on the same football team.

Little by little, Gabriel got Steve out of his suit until he stood before the producer in nothing but his boxer briefs and socks. Steve crossed his arms over his chest anxiously.

"Nice chest," Gabriel remarked. He sat in a chair beside his desk, not behind it. His legs were crossed in a relaxed, easy manner.

"I can shave it if you want," Steve offered.

"No. It's fine. We're looking for real straight guys. That real straight-guy image. It's what our customers like. Can you bottom?"

"Excuse me?"

"Turn around, would you, buddy?"

Steve complied and turned around slowly. He suddenly realized what Gabriel was asking, and his ass cheeks involuntarily clenched.

"Very nice," Gabriel observed. "Can I see it without the briefs?"

Again, Steve assented and bent over, pulling the shorts to the floor.

"Well, I've seen enough," Gabriel said. "Put your clothes back on and we'll get you all set up."

"Cool," Steve said. "Now about the bottoming …"

"If it makes you very uncomfortable, don't worry about it."

"Thanks!" Steve sighed in relief.

"It's just, you can make more money if you bottom. Cliff said you needed the money, so …"

"How much more?"

"Much more," Gabriel assured him. "Much, much more. And you've got one hell of an ass there, Steve. That's a marketable booty." He smiled.

Steve got dressed, and Gabriel led him downstairs to the studio. The whole company was set up in a rather large, old, Greek-style home in what looked like a prestigious neighborhood.

Steve was led past rooms occupied by many young men, and a few women, in various stages of undress and frivolity.

"How many films are you shooting?" Steve asked, mouth agape at what he saw.

"Five, at the moment," Gabriel answered.

They passed by a young man sitting in a camping chair, as a beautiful young woman worked over his private area.

"She's a fluffer," Gabriel explained. "Some guys need a little help to get excited, especially when they're getting ready to fuck someone they wouldn't normally."

"Like another guy."

"Like another guy," Gabriel repeated. "If you ever need one, they're there for you."

"That's okay," Steve said. "I won't need one."

For some reason, he could excuse the indiscretion he was about to do with another man, but he could never cheat on Sandy with another woman. He couldn't explain it, but since the attraction for a man was never there, it didn't matter if a guy sucked him off or … worse.

It was funny how the day started. Just a couple hours before he had kissed Sandy on the cheek, taking in her lavender perfume, and told her he was off to his new job in sales for a video retailer. It wasn't much, and it was only temporary, he had told her, but it paid well. Very well. And she was ecstatic about it. She was finally wearing her carefree smile again.

Steve was handed a long white, robe.

"You can go over there and get undressed," Gabriel said, motioning to a changing room. "But I want you to meet your co-star first."

A well-dressed, handsome man walked over to Steve. He had that same all-American look that Steve was known for; a winning smile, a strong chin, and broad shoulders. The biggest difference was that he was more muscular. He had more brawn, as if he never stopped playing football after college.

"Hi," the man greeted, holding out his hand. "I'm Evan."

"Steve," he introduced himself with a pleasant nod.

"Don't worry," Evan said. "We'll take it easy. The first time is terrifying, I know."

"Have you ever … bottomed?" Steve asked, his voice lowered.

"Absolutely," Evan replied. "There's a lot of money in that. Did it just yesterday."

"All right, bud," Gabriel said. "Let's get you naked." He patted Steve's shoulder affectionately.

Steve undressed, his heart almost ready to burst. As he walked back out onto the set, he felt as if his legs would give out beneath him. He felt as if he had suddenly stepped into a dream. Evan stood near the large queen bed that was to be the setting of Steve's deflowering. He smiled reassuringly at the new gay-for-pay star.

"Okay, Steve," Gabriel said, "let's lose the robe."

Steve let the robe slip from him as he continued walking to Evan.

"Let's have you bend over the bed."

Before he could comply with the request, however, he caught glimpse of the massive piece of meat that was about to be inserted into him. It hung out of Evan's zipper like an angry, starved anaconda.

"Holy shit!" he exclaimed as he stepped backward.

"Don't freak out, man," Evan said. "We'll take it easy. We'll get you into it easy, I promise."

"But how will we get me off of it!"

"Gabe," Evan said. "Maybe you should get someone less endowed for his first time."

"That's a good idea!" Steve pleaded, unable to take his eyes off the monster.

"There's no one else available," Gabriel responded.

"Can you do this?" Evan inquired.

"I-I don't know."

"You need the money, right? Just think about that. Think about who you're doing this for. I've got two little girls I'm trying to raise without a mom. I wouldn't be doing this otherwise. This money's going to put them through school."

Steve nodded and calmed down. "Okay," he said. "But can we get some lube?"

"Of course! You think we're nuts?"

Steve squeezed out a grin. "This is for you and the baby, Sandy," he whispered, taking the requested position on the bed.

Patrick sat in another pair of trunks Cassie had bought for him, his feet dangling over the poolside, as the sound of Jack Johnson filled the air. He had finished early and Cassie insisted he change from his regular clothes and have some fun. It was one of her lunchtime soirees, and the pool area was humming with a few good friends and young gay men Cassie had met at her frequent visits to the local gay night clubs. Patrick watched the men parade around, their bodies postcards for designer underwear and swimming trunks. He watched a well-built Latino change trunks right in front of him, bending over to slide the new pair on.

"I can't believe he just changed right there," he chuckled to Justin, the blonde beside him.

"It's a pageant," Justin said. "Everyday's a pageant."

"It's wild. I love it here."

"You don't mind all these gay guys hitting on you?"

"No," Patrick confessed. "I like it, actually."

They watched the swarthy Latino strut over to Cassie and Becky, who lay stretched out on lounge chairs in bathing suits and sunglasses.

"Damn," Justin observed, "look at the butt!"

"Yeah," Patrick agreed. "Even a straight guy would hit that."

"Wanna dance?" Justin asked as the sunny tunes continued.

"Sure, why not?" Patrick said, as he rose and they started to move to the drums and guitar.

"Woo-hoo!" Cassie yelled from her chair. "You go, Patrick!"

He loved the freedom he felt. He didn't need to worry about saying the wrong thing here. The touch of new experiences made him giddy. He watched the other boys, just a little older than he, and the gay guys from the neighborhood, Terrence, Rick, and David. They were having fun. They were content in their lives, or as content as one could be. They were all comfortable in their own lives, he was sure. He longed for the day when he too would be like that.

The hot Latino walked over to the two young men and began pumping sensually behind Patrick. He smiled at the flirtation. Hoots and hollers rose from the other lunchtime revelers.

Yes, he felt the young man's penis lightly grazing his ass, but it didn't matter. Nothing would come of it, he thought, so why not have fun? It was an experience, one he had never known before, and he embraced it.

"That's what life is all about," Cassie had told him. "In the end, it's the experiences we have that make us who we are, so make sure they're good ones. Find experiences that make you cackle and shriek and ooh and ah. Find the beauty in humanity, in its variety and surprises."

Patrick was in a gay-boy sandwich when Vera, who had risen from her own sunbathing to answer the deafening doorbell, came rushing back and said something to Cassie in a panicked tone. Patrick couldn't hear over the music and distance, but the next thing he knew, Becky was hurrying toward him, the gay boys and neighbors were scattering to the cabana, and Vera and Cassie were rushing into the house.

"What's wrong?" Patrick asked.

"It's your mom, honey," Becky said. "Let's get you inside and changed."

"She's checking up on me," he glowered, as Becky led him into the house and up the back stairs to Jason's room, where his work clothes had been put.

"Well, hello, Melinda!" Cassie exclaimed in faux surprise, as she met her in the foyer. "Won't you come and have a seat in the lounge?" She took Melinda's hand warmly.

"No thank you, Cassie," Melinda said, smiling her appreciative but condescending smile. "I won't be here long. I've just come to see how things are going with Patrick."

"Wonderfully! He's a gem!"

"Really?" Melinda remarked, somewhat surprised.

"Absolutely. He's even agreed to do some other things for me around the house. I pay him extra, of course."

"Oh, I'm so happy it's working out," Melinda said with genuine relief.

"Like bread and butter."

"Hey, Mom," Patrick greeted her, turning the corner on the front stairs. He was dressed, once again, in his white polo and khaki shorts. "What's going on? Do you need me back home?"

"No, darling," she replied. "But, thank you." That was the first time he had ever asked if she needed anything from him. Maybe working for Cassie was doing more good than Melinda had thought it would.

He cleared his throat, breathing heavily.

"Patrick, are you okay?" Melinda inquired. "You look flushed."

"Uh, yeah. I was upstairs moving some things around for Cass-Miss Bloom."

"A cedar chest," Cassie lied. She turned to Patrick. "I told you to wait for Vera or me, silly. You'll hurt yourself."

"Listen to Cassie," Melinda chimed in. "You don't want to pull your back, or herniate something."

"Yes, Mom," Patrick nodded. "Sorry."

"Well, okay then," she said. "I'm going back to the house. Dinner's at six." She turned to leave, and then added, "Oh, and Patrick, turn down that music. I'm sure Cassie doesn't care to hear that blaring through her home."

"It's all right," Cassie remarked. "It's the sound of youth. It's rather nice to hear it in this old house again."

As the door shut behind her, Melinda relief and an odd sense of pride. Patrick seemed to be changing for the better, and who would have thought working for Cassie would bring that about? She almost felt like skipping as she thought of his concern.

"Do you need me?" he had asked. It was the highlight of her day!

She would be able to walk back into her house and tell Nanna that there was nothing wrong, that the suspicions she had been hounding into Melinda were unfounded. Patrick was a good boy, after all!

"He's up to something," Nanna told her that morning, with her bulging eyes squinting. "You better go check on him. That Cassie is a bad influence. She's a Jezebel. A simple whore, and we both know she killed her husband. Why do you let the boy work over there? One might question your mothering abilities."

Mothering abilities, indeed. Melinda was beginning to think the only one with sub par mothering abilities was Nanna herself. Melinda had proof about Patrick. He was a good boy. She had seen it with her own eyes.

Nanna was wrong.

Rick walked from Cassie Bloom's lunch-time get-together feeling good, hopeful even. The sun glinted through the leaves and branches of the large trees along the drive. Birds sang gleeful melodies. If he were the type, it would have been the perfect moment to burst into song. He wouldn't skip, though. There would be absolutely no skipping in Rick's big number.

He walked to James' door wearing his trunks and flip-flops. A towel hung on his shoulder. He was very pleased with how things were going with James. Slow and steady was how Rick liked it. There was no need to rush into anything. Jumping quickly into things had only led to mistakes.

He knocked, and then, without waiting too terribly long, poked his head into the foyer.

"James," he called. No answer. He had told James he would be dropping by, though, so he stepped inside.

Yes, Rick liked how simple their burgeoning relationship was, unencumbered by sex. They had been on four dates, and James was still the perfect gentleman.

"James," Rick called again, walking carefully through hallways full of antiques. His flip-flops smacked on the wood floors.

"Rick. Hey," James greeted, stepping into the hall from the first floor bathroom. He was dripping wet, with a towel wrapped loosely around his waist. "I didn't expect you so early," he said, as steam escaped from the shower.

And just like that, all Rick's former notions about taking things slow were dropped like a bag of bricks.

Rick lunged at James, knocking him against the wall, as he kissed him like he had been wanting to for weeks. James was caught by surprise, but quickly adapted to the situation. He let the towel slip from his body, as Rick licked, bit, and kissed his wet skin. James reciprocated, and ripped Rick's trunks from his body with a grunt. Rick's flip-flops flew off into the air, as he once again tackled the army man.

What occurred next was nothing more than the release of years of pent-up sexual energy, a frenzied free-for-all of various sexual positions and eyebrow-raising noises. They rolled and wrestled and pushed and pulled from room to room, down hallways, over the kitchen table, on the stove, up the stairs, in bed, in the shower, against windows. They demolished innocent antiques and deflowered robust fruits and vegetables.

By the end, the house looked as if it had been visited by a thief or a small cyclone. They lay in each other's arms, breathing heavily, on the kitchen floor in the middle of a messy puddle of whipped cream and mushed bananas.

"Oh my God!" James sighed, exhausted.

"I know."

"Can you believe we just did all of that?"

Rick laughed dryly. "So much for taking it slow," he said. "Half of those positions we just did aren't even possible. What happened to the laws of physics?"

The kitchen phone rang as they lay, not having the energy to rise.

"Are you going to get that?" Rick asked.

"No. I can't move."

"I wore you out, huh?"

"That, and I think there's still a cumquat up my ass."

Rick laughed, jabbing him in the side.

The answering machine picked up the call:

"Jimmy! Jimmy, you there? Fuck it! This is Ballser. I'm comin' into town soon, buddy. I'll try to catch you again tonight. I want to see this new place of yours. We can catch up. Later!"

James was suddenly very quiet.

"Are you okay?" Rick asked. "Who was that?"

"Nobody," James replied. "Just an old army buddy. I'm fine."

The expression on his face said different. His brow furrowed in anxiety and worry. Still, though, he forced a smile, and kissed Rick gently.

"What are we doing in a mall?" Terrence asked, disgust in his voice, as he and David made their way past trendy boutiques and music stores.

"If you want to get Christian a gift, I'm telling you," David said, "he's going to want something new, something that other kids his age like. You know, clothes or music."

"But, David, if he's got my genes, who's to say he won't like something from the places where I love to shop?"

"I have yet to meet a teenage boy who likes to receive gifts that are older than he."

"Look at these kids," Terrence observed. "Who is dressing them? Who is encouraging them to dress like this?"

A pack of Goths passed them on one side, with their dramatic make-up and world-weary expressions; would-be gangstas, with white tanks and baggy jeans, passed on the other.

"I think the Gothic kids are kind of neat," David remarked.

"They can't pull the mournful look off. They've got the make-up right, but their eyes are too young. They haven't seen enough of the shit in the world. Young eyes can never pull off hurt and anger when they're still open to the wonder of the world."

David stared at him. "Wow! That was deep."

"Being a father makes you think, honey."

"Terrence, you've been a dad a whole two-and-a-half weeks."

"That's longer than you, bitch."

His cell phone sang "Everlasting Love," and he picked it from its hip holder. "This is Terrence," he answered. "It's Christian," he side-whispered to David.

David took in his surroundings as Terrence conversed with his son. It was strange to think that some of the kids that surrounded them were the same age as Christian. David suddenly felt a little old. When had he and Terrence ceased to be kids? How did *that* happen?

A gaggle of overly tanned high-school girls walked by, aware of nothing but themselves, passing everyone else with haughty mockery. David rolled his eyes at them. He couldn't help himself. They were clearly victims of a soul-sucking culture.

"Creep!" called out the tannest girl. She would start looking like a piece of rawhide soon if she wasn't careful. She led the others away, and they strutted off in ignorance of their own obvious absurdity.

"Oh, no!" Terrence exclaimed, clicking the phone shut.

David gave him his attention once again, waiting for the newest crisis to unfold.

"He wants to visit! He wants to visit before the summer's out!"

"You're going to meet your boy, Dad," David said, wrapping an arm around his neck.

Steve drove back home in contemplation of the day's peculiar events. Who would have thought it? Steve Jones, a gay porn star. Well, not a star yet, but Gabriel had assured him, "With an ass like that, you can make serious money."

That was the strangest thing anybody had ever said to him, bar none!

As he passed banks, shopping centers, and law offices, his mind was still in the studio. It was surreal to him. Had he really spent the morning being screwed up the butt by another man? Of course, there was no denying it. The pain in the beginning was intense. He had wanted to cry. But as things progressed, something happened. There was unbelievable pleasure as Evan's large penis hit something deep inside him over and over, and, in the end, Steve came all over the place.

And it was all caught on film!

That was the scariest thought. That his deflowering, as it were, was to be viewed by millions of people over the internet and on DVD. The thought frightened him so much that he was tempted to grab the camera and run out the studio door towards the nearest incinerator. But then Gabriel showed him his check, and fearful thoughts were quieted, if just a little.

"I get paid all this for letting some guy screw me?" he asked, looking incredulously at the producer.

"And you can make more, too. One of our other new guys backed out of his shoot. How would you like to fill in? It's only a jack-off scene, so the pay isn't as good, but it's more cash."

"My ass gets a rest?"

"Your hot ass gets a rest."

So, Steve did his second porn video in one day. The gay-for-pay business was becoming a lucrative opportunity for him.

He finished the scene, grabbed his check, and headed home.

"We'll get hold of you," Gabriel assured him.

Steve stopped by his bank on his way back to Sandy and deposited the checks. His mind-and ass-felt half numb.

Sandy was waiting on him as usual as he drove into the drive.

"Hey, baby!" she gleamed, running to him with her arms wide open. Sometimes she could seem like a stereotype from an old black-and-white TV series.

He kissed her passionately. "It's good to be home," he said.

"How was the first day?" she asked.

"Interesting," he replied. "Very interesting. I think I'm going to do well. And it'll even allow me time to look for another job."

"Wonderful!" Sandy exclaimed, grabbing his ass playfully. She didn't notice the slight look of discomfort on his face.

Patrick counted through the money again, and placed it back into the envelope. He then placed that into a Skechers shoebox, which he placed in the back of the closet shelf. He kept a running record of how much he brought home each afternoon, and it was adding up quickly and nicely. He was sure Cassie was paying him too much, way too much. But as long as she was fine with it, who was he to say anything?

He saved all the money. Not a dime was spent on CDs or clothes. He had bigger aspirations. Instant gratification would need to wait until he had time for it. He was saving to get out, to get a car and then a job. If college was in his future at all, he was going to need to work for it. His parents would not help.

"College is worldly and promotes dangerous lifestyles," Melinda chided. "Your father and I never attended college, and we're fine. We live in a lovely house, and your father has a great job. Plus, we've got the respect of the neighborhood. They know how much we've had to work to get where we are."

How could he ever expect her to understand?

"Patrick," his mother called from downstairs. "Dinner's ready!"

He shut the closet door, and, as he stepped into the hallway, he nearly knocked over Nanna.

"Watch where you're going!" she groused.

"Sorry," he mumbled. *Had she been standing there the whole time?*

"No, you're not."

"Smelly old bitch," he insulted her under his breath.

"What?" she shouted. "What did you say?"

He didn't respond, but only smiled as he descended the steps.

CHAPTER 8

Gabriel had set Steve up in one of the six small rooms in the back of the house. Each of these rooms, no larger than a small office, was decorated with props to resemble a certain environment. Steve sat in front of the computer in "The CEO Room." He was dressed in a very distinguished suit and tie, an ensemble that would quickly be shed as soon as his show began.

He had the 10:30 slot. Gabriel told him it might be a permanent gig if the numbers were good. It was a quick way to earn an extra thousand while he was needed on the set. The studio, he observed, was nothing more than a factory. It churned out more porn than he had ever seen and was becoming one of the most profitable companies of its kind because of the quick turnaround and the respect with which the stars were treated.

"You're on in 5 ..." came a kind female voice through a loud speaker.

He readied himself. This would be his first time on webcam, and he had to admit it was exciting. The idea of being watched while doing something so intimate gave him an instant hard-on.

Steve signed on. A password had been given to him, and he soon saw an image of himself reflected on the screen via a tiny camera attached to the monitor. To make it less awkward for the actor, music played through the speaker, something jazzy and seductive.

As soon as Steve was given the signal, he began leering into the camera like Evan had shown him. To take away the tension, he pretended he was trying to seduce Sandy. He rubbed at his chest and crotch as messages scrolled up the bottom of the screen.

"Fuck yeah, man!"

"Rip that shirt off, bitch!"

"Fuck me, Daddy! Fuck me!"

It was crazy! They loved it. They were getting off to his every move. It made him incredibly hard. Even if they were guys, they were guys getting off to him. Thousands of them.

When he whipped out his dick the screen went nuts. The messages scrolled so quickly he was unable to read any of them. But the masturbatorial frenzy it sent him into soon led to an orgasm like he had never known. He fell back into his chair, exhausted. He flashed a cocky grin at the camera as a thousand "thank yous" and marriage proposals scrolled up.

Before the session was terminated Steve caught a familiar screen name sign on.

Fitking04: That was hot, Steve! Cliff says you're going to be a star!

Instead of being humiliated that David and Cliff had seen his performance, Steve was relieved that he had passed muster. His congratulatory self-recognition was short-lived, however, as the guilt set in.

"Are you sure about this, Terrence?" James asked.

"Positive," Terrence answered. "As a father, I should be able to play football with my son. In order to do that, I need to be taught the game. You love football. Therefore, who better to teach me?"

James looked to Rick for some back-up. The three of them stood in James' backyard. It was a sizeable patch of lawn, with a brick walkway down the middle leading to a small replica of the Fountain of the Four Rivers.

"He's set," Rick shrugged. "He'll bail out anyway."

"I won't!"

"Well, at least he's dressed for it," James said.

And, in truth, Terrence was. He wore his GAP t-shirt, his Old Navy sweatpants, and a red bandanna.

"Bring it!" he said, squatting into a stance he had seen the players take on TV.

James spun the ball in his hand. "Let's go you a little farther. I'll practice throwing it."

"Throwing?" Terrence quipped. "Anyone can throw! I want the blood and guts of the game. Let's practice tackling." he grinned at Rick. "Do you mind me tackling your *loooover*?"

"I'm the teacher here," James said as he sprinted to the edge of the yard. "We do it how I say. Got it?"

"Whatever," Terrence grumbled.

Surprisingly, Terrence wasn't too bad at catching the ball. He fumbled once or twice, but his skill rather impressed both James and Rick.

"Now can we tackle?" Terrence asked, throwing the ball to the grass.

"Fine," James gave in. "Let's switch places first, though. I need to talk to Rick."

"Yippee!" Terrence hollered as he passed James on the grass.

"Okay," James instructed. "I'm going to throw the ball to you, and then you run toward me with it."

"Easy sleazy!"

"What did you need to talk to me about?" Rick asked.

"Hold on," James answered. The ball was in flight, caught perfectly by Terrence. They raced at each other, but Terrence grew cautious at the last minute.

"You can't do that. You see? You got scared. You've got to focus. Let's try it again. This time you throw to me."

James jogged back to Rick. "It's about my friend, Ballser."

"What about him?"

"Well, he's difficult for some people to take."

Terrence threw the football and James easily caught it. Yet, he stood beside Rick, trying to explain his friend Ballser.

"Hey!" Terrence yelled. "Aren't you going to run at me?"

James ignored the shout. "You see, Ballser ... he's a pretty thoughtless guy ..."

"Hey!" Terrence shouted again, his hands placed on his hips.

"How do you mean?" Rick asked.

"He's ..."

"Hey!" Terrence screamed.

"Dammit!" James roared, as he took off to tackle Terrence without the ball.

"Aaaaah!"

Melinda could finally breathe. Figuratively, of course. She could at last relax in the aisles of the supermarket. She had managed to sneak out of the house, for once, without Nanna. There was a twinge of guilt, but Melinda simply had to have some time to herself.

She chided herself for being miffed at Nanna, but miffed she was! Anyone would be! Why, that very morning Nanna had snooped around.

"I threw away that filth you had hidden upstairs! You should be ashamed of yourself!" Nanna scolded.

Melinda was perplexed. "What are you talking about, Mother?"

"I found that tape. The one with that woman bouncing all around with barely a stitch on. It was on the shelf by the desk. I got rid if it!"

"Mother! That was my new workout tape! *Ann Coulter's Right-robics*, not porn!"

"Well, it looked dirty to me."

Melinda was truly, truly … miffed. She had to get out of the house. Once Nanna hit the bathroom, she knew it was her chance. The bathroom was always an ordeal for Nanna. Actually, Nanna's trips to the bathroom were an ordeal for the whole family. The noises coming from the small room were grotesque and frightening.

In the supermarket, Melinda felt at ease. She could focus on other, more pleasant things.

"Blackberry frappucinos?" she chuckled, picking up a carton. "What will they think of next?"

As she continued down the aisle, stopping and starting every few steps, she felt like she was being watched. She was always able to tell when someone was watching her. God had given her that ability, no doubt to help her in some great deed that was yet to come.

Two tank-top sporting, scraggly-haired teenagers grinned at her suggestively. She smiled in embarrassed acknowledgment.

"Can I help you boys?" she asked. They were most likely in the wrong aisle, and needed someone to direct them appropriately.

"You bet you can!" one of teenagers answered.

"Damn, woman!" the other added. "You are a total MILF!"

"Excuse me?"

"A Mom I'd Like to Fuck. How about it?"

In utter shock, Melinda sped her cart around and headed away from the leering boys as they called after her.

A MILF? Was she a MILF?

She stood, breathing hard, at the poultry. She opened the freezer doors to cool off. She couldn't help but smile.

There it was. Proof that she was still attractive. Those teenage boys had flirted with her. How rude, and yet amazing! A small laugh escaped from her lips.

Patrick placed the last of the college brochures Cassie had procured for him down on the end table. It was a wonderful thought, the idea of actually attending college. But it almost seemed an impossibility, a fairytale. Melinda would never allow it. Still, Cassie was kind to have thought of him.

He rose from the couch and wandered about the house. The Bloom house was almost three times as large as the other houses in the neighborhood. Of course, that was due to the fact that it had been on the spot much longer than the neighborhood. It was the House on the Hill, as far as everyone was concerned, peering out over the suburban wilderness that was the Bloom keep.

Patrick was still finding little rooms and passageways throughout the house. Cassie was fine with his adventuring. She encouraged it.

"I'm the last person to step in front of an inquisitive mind," she said.

He found the basement door behind a great potted fern. Its leaves branched out in operatic opulence. He moved it aside carefully, making sure not to scuff the floor. His curiosity getting the better of him, he pulled at the doorknob which opened without resistance. He quickly found a light switch and descended the old stairs into the cool air of the underground.

There were no cobwebs to swat aside, nor any curious odors. Other than the low ceiling, it was actually a rather comfortable environment. Like most basements, the Blooms' was used for storage. Yet, unlike others, Cassie seemed to have much more to store. In fact, the memorabilia, furniture, old paintings draped in cloth, and nondescript crates stretched on for rows unending. It was like a gallery or a museum. And there were other rooms as well. The basement was much larger in area than the rest of the house, stretching back to the land behind the house.

Patrick spent a while investigating all he saw. Because of the unbelievable amount of items being stored there, he knew that his adventuring in the basement had just begun.

As he continued down the corridor of rooms, the light dimmed dramatically. The rooms, filled with desks and tables, looked like offices. They had a hard, unfeeling quality to them. It unnerved him.

The only room with a closed door lay at the very end of the corridor. Still, when Patrick turned the knob, the door opened easily. His eyes sought to adjust as he peered into the dark room. Then, suddenly, he saw the glint of the white of eyes. He stumbled backward, falling onto the concrete floor.

He gained his composure and stood again, seeing the eyes were those of a portrait. It was Jackson Bloom, looking severe and emotionless.

Patrick ventured stealthily into the room. Unlike the others, this room was filled with things of a more personal nature, not desks and chairs. Mr. Bloom's suits, wrapped in plastic, hung on a long pipe that jutted out from a corner.

There was a box filled with pictures. Patrick suddenly realized that there were no photographs of Jackson Bloom in the house above. He realized that the reason for that was because they were all here.

Most of the pictures were of Jackson alone, but there were some with Cassie. As Patrick flipped through them, he found only one with Jason. But that made sense. Jason's face could be seen all over the house, in practically every room.

"I was wondering how long it would take you to come down here."

Cassie's smooth voice startled Patrick. He dropped the photo back in the box.

"Don't worry, sweetie," she assured him. "You're fine. I never lock the basement. You're free to look around."

"What is all of this?" he asked. "All these rooms?"

Cassie stared at him, a wrinkle appearing on her brow.

"Let's just say that Mr. Bloom was not the wonderful man many people in this town made him out to be." She chose not too delve too deeply into that particular understatement. Jackson Bloom was a many of many interests and talents. And one of his many secretive charges by the higher-ups in the government was sanctioned human experimentation on vagrants and runaways. Suburbia was the perfect cover for this.

"You kept all of his things?"

"I suppose I just haven't found the courage to get rid of him-let go of him-completely yet."

She walked closer to Patrick. "I made some fresh cookies upstairs. Why don't you go have some."

"Sure," Patrick said. "Ms. Bloom ..."

"Cassie," she corrected.

"Cassie. I'm sorry. I didn't mean to intrude. I was just curious."

"Never apologize for satisfying your curiosity."

He turned and headed back the corridor and up the stairs.

Cassie turned and looked into the box. She picked up the photo of Jason.

"How'd I miss this one?" she whispered, then walked out of the room with the photo. She closed the door behind her.

CHAPTER 9

Rick rose from the breakfast table at hearing the doorbell.

He had been staying over at James' house on and off for two weeks. It was becoming a comfortable routine. He would wake up and kiss James on his unshaven cheek, then carefully crawl out of bed so as not to wake him. He would wrap the first article of clothing he could find around him, usually one of James' oversized army shirts, and go downstairs to make breakfast and coffee.

Rick still was unable to bring himself to remove his eye patch. Despite their intimacy, James hadn't seen him without it.

James would soon wake to the smell of coffee and frying bacon, and descend the stairs himself in his boxers, groggy and bleary-eyed. Since he was beginning to grow his hair back, it stuck up in all sorts of angles. Even after a shower it was hard to tame.

"Another advantage of the army," he said.

Rick would set him a plate and accept a morning kiss on the mouth. Then, they would sit, just the two of them, flipping through the paper or watching the morning shows.

There was a pleasant oddness to feeling like an old married couple. Rick was beginning to understand the lure of conformity and routine.

"You two are so getting hitched," Terrence would tease.

After James had revived a bit more, he would shuffle off to take a shower, leaving Rick at the table until he would come bounding into the kitchen again, wet and frisky. Rick was waiting for the welcome attack when the doorbell had rung.

He opened the door and was confronted by an intimidating bully of a man who looked Rick up and down with unappreciative eyes.

"Who are you?" the man asked gruffly.

Rick suddenly felt more self-conscious than usual. He tugged at the bottom of his borrowed shirt, making certain it was covering his nakedness beneath.

"Rick. I'm Rick," he answered, holding out a hand.

The man ignored the gesture and pushed his way into the house.

"Where's Jimmy?" he asked, looking around.

"In the shower. He should be out soon."

"What? Do you clock his showers?" He looked at Rick with suspicion.

"You must be Ballser," Rick said. He had decided he did not like the man very much.

"Yeah," the man curtly replied. "I'm Ballser." He paused and scratched his head. "Excuse me, Rick," he said. "But what exactly are you doing standing half naked in Jimmy's house with Jimmy's shirt touching your junk? Don't seem quite right to me."

The sound of large, running feet pounded through the house and into the kitchen before Rick could answer the asshole's question.

"Ricky! Where are you?" James yelled mischievously.

Rick gave Ballser a weak smile, as the army man looked at him with confusion.

"Ricky!" James called again, coming into the foyer in search. Rick breathed a sigh of relief that he was at least sporting a towel.

James froze, staring from Ballser to Rick.

"Ballser!" he said in shock disguised (though not very well) as happiness. "You're early."

"Yeah, just thought I'd come by as soon as possible so we could get our party going." He walked to James, hitting him on the shoulder. "I'd give you a hug, but I ain't a fag, you know," he joked.

James caught Rick's eyebrow raise in disgust at the word … and the man.

"Nice place you got here, Jimmy." He wandered around the room, inspecting things. "But who's the guy standing around in your t-shirt?" He looked at Rick as if he expected James to be looking at him the same way.

Rick could see James' mind fumbling around for excuses. He looked to Rick for help.

"I'm his gardener," Rick lied irritably. "I took care of the lawn when his uncle was here."

"Why are you in Jimmy's shirt?" It didn't seem like he was buying it.

"Uh, he fell into the fountain out back," James spoke up. "I let him borrow that until his clothes are cleaned and dried."

The answer satisfied the Neanderthal. "Well, you might have given him some pants, chief," Ballser remarked. "Where do I set my shit?" he asked, changing the subject, oblivious to the great relief of everybody else in the room.

"There's an extra room, upstairs, to the left, three doors down. I'll be up as soon as I get dressed."

"Fan-fuckin'-tastic!" Ballser replied, as he climbed the stairs. "Then we can get to the drinking. Just you and me, like old times."

When he had turned the corner at the top of the stairs, and was safely out of sight or hearing range, James took hold of Rick by the shoulders. "Shit," he said. "I'm sorry. I should have warned you about him."

"They should have town criers for people like that," Rick grumbled.

"Can we keep us quiet? At least around him?" James asked. "He's not the first person I want to tell."

"I don't blame you, but James ..."

"I know. I love you, Ricky. I do. And soon everyone will know it. But I want it to be known in my way, okay? Not from some loud-mouthed bigot."

The proclamation of love caught Rick by surprise.

"I thought he was your friend," he fumbled out.

"*Was*," James emphasized. "Past tense. He can't get past his glory days, because his life is such shit right now. Can you just hold on for me? It'll just be a few days."

"Of course, I will," Rick said. "You two have fun tonight. I'll go get my stuff."

"Thanks, baby." He kissed him quickly on the cheek. "I'll call you tonight," he promised as he raced off for his room, trailing water behind him.

Nanna made the decision that Patrick's uppity attitude needed to be fixed. Since she knew Melinda was not going to take any action, it was up to her to get things done. Nanna knew she was the true matriarch, after all.

She pretended to be asleep on the sofa, the television showing muted, black-and-white scenes of old movies. As soon as Patrick left the house, she pulled her summer sweater over her head and waited until she was certain he was a good distance away before heading out herself. She was intent on watching his every move, all day long. She would catch him. She knew he was up to something. Melinda was simply too naive to see it. She could be such a stupid girl at times, trusting her faithless son to work for an immoral murderess. Why, this was the Devil working in their very neighborhood!

The first part of the morning was uneventful. Nanna spied as Patrick cleaned the pool of leaves and picked up anything out of place around the pool area. There was nothing peculiar about that, though he did seem to be having a good time. That was troubling.

Things changed when Cassie came out and said something to him. Nanna tried to listen more intently, but she was too far away. She couldn't make out a thing they were saying.

"Crap," she muttered, and again disturbed a bird in a nearby bush by passing a loud whistle of gas.

She watched Cassie put her arm around Patrick's shoulder as they walked into the house. Nanna attempted to escape from the bushes without making too much noise, but that was a little difficult. Her foot got caught on a root, and she fell backward onto sticky pine needles.

"Lord have mercy!" she griped.

When she finally found her way out of the manicured bushes and trees, she carefully looked from window to window until she at last found Patrick and Cassie in a large room with a television. Nanna scoffed at the obscenely large screen. Secretly, though, she wondered how Bogie and Bacall might look on it. Why, it was practically the size of a cinema screen!

She watched her grandson with harsh eyes. What was this about? Why was he inside instead of outside working?

She smiled, thinking that she might have hit the jackpot, and stood on the edge of a cinder block beside the window where she had a better view.

Patrick sat comfortably on the large, black, suede sofa. Cassie brought him a glass of lemonade and some cookies. It surprised him at first that Vera didn't do more of the cooking and housecleaning. That was her job, wasn't it? Wasn't she the maid?

"Not really," Cassie had explained. "Vera's a friend. I helped her out a few years ago, and so she helps me out here."

"Does she live here?"

"She has a room here, but she has an apartment in the city as well, near the club she owns."

"She owns a club?"

"Yes," Cassie answered. "The same club where I met your new friend Justin."

"What's it called?"

"*Vera's*," Cassie said, as if it were a silly question.

"I think I'd like to go some time."

"We shall," she agreed. "And so we shall."

Vera was gone for the day, however, as Patrick sat with Cassie in the TV room. She was dressed in a white GAP t-shirt and pink slacks. Her feet were bare and the nails painted a bashful rose. She crossed her legs and turned on the television.

"So what do you need my help with?" Patrick asked. On brief occasions he was afraid his situation with Cassie would turn into a creepy Mrs. Robinson thing. He couldn't imagine Cassie trying to seduce him, though. Besides, she knew there was a girl in school he was interested in, and she was constantly urging him to make a move on her.

"Patrick," Cassie said, turning to him, one hand playing with her hair. "Have you ever watched porn?"

He was a little thrown by the question. "Uh, no," he answered, swallowing some lemonade.

"None of any kind? Not even on the internet?"

"Are you kidding? Mom had those blockers put on first thing. I don't think I even saw another person's naked butt until I started working here and that Spanish dude changed in front of everyone."

"Would you have a problem with watching some?"

"I don't think so," he replied.

"Not even gay porn? You wouldn't be uncomfortable with watching that?"

"Definitely not," he said. He was actually kind of interested to see what it was gay guys did. "Why are you asking?"

"Because that is what I need your help with. Vera normally helps me select the play list, but since she's busy ..."

"Play list for what?" he asked, reaching for a sugar cookie.

"For my annual gay porn party."

Patrick smiled broadly. "Seriously?"

She returned the expression. "Seriously. What do you say? I can pay you extra."

He shrugged. "Cool," he said, with a mouthful of cookie. "Let's watch some dick."

Cassie laughed. "Wonderful!"she exclaimed.

She pushed play on the DVD wand, and the first film began. *Booty and the Beast.*

"This one is supposed to have the best gay three-way of all last year. It won a Golden Prostate."

"They have awards?"

"You bet they do! And they deserve them. Do you realize how many straight women get pointers from gay porn? And besides," she added, "it's just hot! I've got some popcorn and other snacks. Make yourself comfy. We've got a lot of blow jobs and butt sex to go through."

Patrick giggled at her bluntness as the first reels of the film began.

Nanna observed the interaction between Cassie and Patrick with a gritting resentment. It made her sick and angry.

Why was that harlot sitting so close to her grandson? He was a brat, sure, but he was her brat to set right! The moment Cassie touched him, Nanna would break into that room and whisk Patrick back home. Then she would make sure Melinda sent him to church camp for the summer. After that ... well, there had to be some way to nip his nastiness in the bud, to lobotomize it from him. Did shock therapy work?

But Cassie never touched him. Instead, she turned on the giant TV and a film began to play. Some badly made romance, from the looks of it. The costumes were cheap, the sets hardly realistic. It seemed to be set in France or Italy. Some very un-American place. She couldn't tell. But the brawny, muscular man who entered the scene definitely got her attention. His shirtless torso was sweaty and hard, most likely after a long day's work. He was a fine looking man. The men of her day never looked like that. Such arms! Such strength! A provider if she ever saw one.

Then another man came into frame. He, too, was strapping and handsome. Nanna felt a sudden prickling in her skin.

What was going on? She hadn't felt like this for years?

Her breath began to steam up the window as she leaned in closer. The two were most likely fighting for the attention of the same woman. Maybe it wasn't such a bad film after all.

Suddenly, the first man pushed the other man down, and undid his pants, and ...

"Oh, my lord!" Nanna gasped.

Her sudden shock caused her to lose her balance on the cinder block, and she fainted backward, onto the grass.

Sandy stood in the doorway with Steve's arms wrapped around her in a tight embrace. The room was coming along wonderfully. She was making plans already, designing mobiles and choosing colors in her mind. The baby would have the perfect room waiting for it upon arrival.

"We're going to have a happy baby," Sandy sighed.

"The happiest baby in the world," Steve whispered in her ears. "It'll be spoiled for sure."

"Steve, I think you should keep this new job," she said.

"What?" he asked, taken off guard. She wanted him to keep bending over for other guys? But she didn't know that's what he did, did she?

"This sales position," she explained. "I think you should keep it. Let's not worry about trying to find something new."

He coughed nervously. "Why?"

"You're doing so well there, and they're so good about hours. You would definitely be able to spend more time with the baby than most fathers. It's just a great situation, don't you think?"

"Uh, yeah. Definitely," he replied. "The situation is ... great."

"I didn't think jobs like that existed. It's a godsend."

Steve held onto her, trying to stifle his anxious breathing. He felt as if his heart was going to explode. If he were to tell her, would she ever understand? Would she see that it was all for her and the baby?

The doorbell rang, momentarily assuaging Steve's meltdown.

"I'll get it," he said, relieved to be free of the moment.

He left the room and walked slowly downstairs, pondering his problem the whole way. He should try to tell her. Somehow he had to let her know. But it had to be in a gentle manner. There had to be a way to soften the blow.

Hey, honey, I get my prostate checked on a weekly basis ... and they pay me for it! Isn't that great?

As Steve opened the door, Hot UPS Guy stood there, his face bowed in humiliation. His last visit to the Jones residence had resulted in less than happy memories. He handed Steve a thin, cardboard package and an electronic form to sign. There was no way he was going to make eye contact.

Steve nodded, appreciating the discomfort of the moment. "How's your, uh ..."

"It's good!" Hot UPS Guy snapped. "It's fine! A few stitches, that's it."

"So, you can ...?"

"Yes. It's fine," he repeated, irritably.

"Well ... that's ... good ..."

Steve handed him the electronic form, and Hot UPS Guy took it without hesitation before walking rapidly to the large brown van and speeding away as quickly as possible. Gayhound took off after the vehicle.

He tore into the package immediately, having some idea what it might be. Gabriel had promised to send him a copy of his latest DVD so that Steve could study it. His star was rising, and he wanted to see if there was room for improvement in his performances. What could he do better? What could he do to earn more money for Sandy and the baby?

Looking at the cover of *Bodybuilder Butt Buddies in Business,* he was struck again with the thought that people he had known, people he had gone to school with, might get hold of the DVD. It was completely possible that some- one he knew would one day see him being pumped full of another man's jism. It was completely possible that some people already had. What would his foot- ball coach back in college think?

Steve swallowed as he regarded the cover. There he was, the star player, leer- ing at the camera as a titan of a man stood behind him suggestively. Yes, Steve was definitely taking one for the team.

In the past couple of weeks he had become somewhat paranoid about the matter. He imagined everyone knew but Sandy, and they were judging him, looking down on him. He knew this was a ridiculous notion, but it never failed to surface when he went out. The guy at the video store the previous night had seemed especially friendly. Could he have …?

He heard Sandy descending the stairs, so he quickly searched for a tempo- rary hiding place. He spotted a basket under the foyer table. Sandy must have just placed it there as decor. He hid the DVD underneath what looked like blankets just as Sandy came into the room.

"Who was that, hon?" she asked.

"Oh, no one," he lied. "They were just lost. People are always getting lost in this neighborhood?"

Sandy carried the large, wicker basket down the sidewalk to Cassie Bloom's majestic abode at the end of the street. She had completely forgotten about the linens and tablecloths she had borrowed for the costume party on the Fourth of July, storing them in the basket by the door. She had meant to return them the very next day, but, due to the pressing money concerns at the time, had for- gotten they were even there. Thankfully things were much better now.

She breathed in the scent of mowed lawns and summer. It was a beautiful day, a beautiful life. Everything was going so well. She was afraid that, at any moment, the dam would break and something would give. But she tried to erase those thoughts from her mind. Everything was fine, and she should try and enjoy it.

She rang the doorbell, glancing around the full-length porch with admiration. What a lovely place, she thought. She wondered if she and Steve would ever be able to afford a place like this. He was making significantly more money. It wasn't out of the question that they might be able to move to a larger home in a few years, maybe even one with a pool. That would certainly make her Fourth of July parties more entertaining. She smiled at the fantasy.

As she waited, she heard a struggle in the bushes at the side of the house, and left the door to investigate. Melinda's mother stumbled into view, as if she were drunk or just waking up and hadn't found her morning feet yet. Sandy didn't know the woman at all, but she knew enough about her to surmise that she was no friend of Cassie's. What, then, was she doing at her home?

The old woman seemed to be surprised to see Sandy, and then the look instantly changed to one of threat. Sandy would have been terrified if she believed in the old superstition about the "evil eye" killing anyone it gazed upon.

The old woman struggled quickly onto the sidewalk, and scurried back to Melinda's, glancing over her shoulder every now and then as Sandy watched her go.

The door opened, and Sandy turned around again to face the door. Patrick stood facing her.

"Hi, Patrick," Sandy greeted, cheerfully. "Cassie's got you butlering, huh?"

"I guess," he shrugged with a grin.

"I brought the tablecloths back that I borrowed from Cassie for the Fourth. Tell her I'm sorry it took so long." She handed the basket to Patrick.

"Will do," he replied. "Thanks."

"Oh, and Patrick," she said before leaving. "I think your grandmother might have been spying on you. I just saw her leave from the side of the house. Just warning you. I know you're having some problems … not that it's any of my business."

A look of fear came over his face, as his eyes widened. "Thanks," he said again.

Patrick absentmindedly carried the basket into the TV room, a knot of dread growing in the pit of his stomach.

"Sandy brought your tablecloths back," he said, in a detached tone, as Cassie lazed on the sofa.

"Would you put those in the wash room for me, darling?" Cassie requested. "I'll get to them later."

"Sure."

"Are you all right, sweetie?"

"Yeah, I'm fine," Patrick replied, shaking off his fear.

He took the basket to the wash room, and instinctively started unpacking it, his mind elsewhere. Near the bottom he found a DVD. It looked like another porn. He barely glanced at the naked men on the cover.

Would Nanna tell Melinda? Of course she would! That old bitch had nothing but hate for him.

"I found this one in the basket," Patrick said, holding up the DVD in his hand as he walked back to the TV room.

"Just put it in the pile. I doubt we'll get to it today, though."

Patrick placed the DVD into Cassie's "pile o' porn" and sat back down on the sofa.

"Are you sure you're okay?" Cassie asked. "You seem a bit distracted."

"I'm fine," Patrick reiterated. "Just thinking about my grandmother, that's all."

"Then I see why you're suddenly depressed." She turned off *Forrest Rump*. "Let's go get some ice cream," she suggested.

"What?"

"You look like you need some ice cream. Let's go." She stood, pulling him up.

He finally smiled as she wrapped an arm around his shoulder before they walked from the room.

Terrence sat studying the woman who was once the girl he had made a baby with years ago. She had changed only slightly. She had added a few pounds, her eyes no longer holding youthful dreams, but she had the same spirit, the same soul. She smiled pleasantly, the sun playing with her straight, auburn hair as they sat at an outside table at a café. The cars and pedestrians passed them by without notice, solitary worlds in a crowded universe.

The woman, Tessa, sipped her iced tea as Terrence played with the salad he had ordered. He had yet to take a bite. It would probably go to waste. He could never eat when his nerves got to him ... but he could drink. It was too bad the café only offered soft drinks, tea, or water.

"So," she began after an unbearable silence. "How have you been, Terrence?"

"I've been good," he replied, his nervousness apparent. "Why did you want to meet?"

"Oh, good. To the point."

"Is it about Christian? I can't imagine it being about anything else." His eyes suddenly widened, and he sat up straight. "Are you looking for alimony!"

"No," she laughed. "Nothing like that. I just wanted to check you out. That's all."

"Check me out?"

"Well, if Chris is going to be getting to know you, I'm guessing I should reacquaint myself with you as well."

"But there's something else, isn't there?"

"Yes," she admitted. "There is."

Terrence stared at her defiantly. "I'm still gay, Tessa. That hasn't changed. I was gay even then, but I didn't want to admit it to myself. But if you think that's going to keep me from seeing my son, you've got another think coming, missy! I'm his father. I have the right to see him, and your religion can't destroy blood ties. It may be able to destroy lives, but not blood ties. Nothing can do that!"

Tessa reached across the table and took his hand gently. "Terrence, calm down. I have no intention of keeping you two apart. I'm happy you want to be part of his life."

"Oh," he said as he settled down. "But I thought ..."

"I knew you were gay when we conceived Chris. I think everybody knew, but you. I was just one of those girls who thought I could change the gay guy."

"Everybody knew?"

He was shocked, and she was shocked that he was shocked.

"Terrence, honey, I'm sorry, but how could they not? You're very obvious." She patted his hand affectionately. "Your being gay never mattered to me. I'm a religious woman, yes, but I believe God doesn't create anything flawed. Therefore, God must have made you just as you are. As gay as the day is long. There's a reason behind everything."

"I don't know what to say," he said, feeling an odd appreciation for her at the moment. "So why are we here?"

"I just wanted to see what kind of dad you might turn out to be," she answered. "And it looks like you're going to be a great one. I was hoping you wouldn't turn out to be a drug addict. That was my worst fear."

"Thanks ... I think. Was that a compliment?" He glanced at her awkwardly. "I do drink, Tessa. I can really put it back sometimes."

Tessa shrugged. "Who doesn't drink?" She paused. "He's a great kid, Terry. We have a great son."

"I know we do. I can tell. Our conversations are very ... deep."

"And he's caring. Everything strikes wonder in him. He wants to join the Peace Corps, you know?" Her pride was infectious.

"Really?"

"You're going to love him."

"I already do." He felt as if he were going to cry. Were those tears? Real tears?

"Does he know I'm gay?" Terrence asked. It was a loaded question, he knew.

"I don't know," Tessa answered. "I don't think it would matter. All he's said from his conversations with you is that he thinks you're cool, and ..."

"And what?"

"And that your voice sounded weird." She giggled. "Are you trying to butch up, Terrence?"

"Shut up," he said, picking at his salad again. "Tessa, answer me this."

"What?" she asked, leaning forward on the table.

"If I were to get him a gift, would he be more excited about an ipod or, say, an antique reading lamp?"

Rick sat on his bed, his back against the headboard, the phone in hand. He was still in his trunks.

He had kept to himself for most of the day since leaving James earlier.

Ballser. What kind of name was Ballser?

The house was quiet. The TV in the next room was silent for once. Terrence had left to spend some time with Christian's mother and had not yet returned. They would probably make a night of it, catching up on the years. David was in his own room, finishing up an article for one of the gay magazines for which he freelanced. Only Rick was alone with his own breathing and his fears.

The solitude and quiet only made Rick more nervous. He felt a familiar dread. It was the same feeling he had whenever Coby would stay out late. He was powerless to prevent whatever trouble or disaster was about to occur. Life controlled him, not the other way around. He had given up trying to make sense of it. At times, he felt like a rubber ball, thrown around endlessly by impacts on harsh surfaces. And then the one time Coby had taken Rick along with him, Rick had lost his eye.

"C'mon, Baby," Coby had pleaded. "I'll take care of you."

In retrospect, Rick should have known better. The bar where they went was a rough place, and Coby had too many debts to have any business going into a place like that. It shouldn't have surprised either of them that one of Coby's debtors would be there and would want his money. What did surprise Rick was how easily Coby forgot about him; how quickly his earlier promise was forgotten. Even before Coby ducked in front of him and the pool cue was rammed into Rick's eye, he knew he and Coby were through. Rick heard, "Baby, Baby, I'm sorry," all the way to the hospital. But that wouldn't save his eye.

James had promised he would call, but it was getting late, almost eleven, and Rick still hadn't heard from him. He could take the waiting no longer, and hit the speed dial. It rang twice before James picked it up.

"Hello," he answered. Rick could hear Ballser in the background, yelling some incoherent insult.

"James. It's me.," Rick said. He felt better already, just from hearing the sound of James' voice. "I'm just checking in. How is everything?"

James sighed. "Ballser's drunk off his ass." He lowered his tone, and Rick could hear Ballser's rants becoming less audible as James fled to another part of the house.

"I can tell."

"I'm sorry I haven't called," James apologized. "He's been a handful. I keep hoping he'll pass out, but I forgot what a drinker he was. Seems his tolerance has doubled since the last time we drank together."

"Jimmy!" Ballser screamed from a few feet away, having followed his host. "Come on!"

"I'll be back in a minute, man. This is important."

Rick smiled at that affirmation.

"So you're not going to be able to get rid of him?" Rick asked.

"No. And there's more. It's not good."

"What?" Rick knew his bad luck was sticking around.

"He needs a place to stay ... for a while."

"You didn't!"

"Rick, I had to. We were buddies."

"You *were* buddies. You've already pointed that out. That's all past."

"I'm sorry, Rick. I've got to help him. It's a brotherhood thing." He paused, readying a better explanation. "He saved my life, Rick. That gash on my thigh. It could have been a lot worse if he wasn't there."

Rick knew he had no right to say anything. Especially not after what he had just been told. They had, in fact, just begun dating a few weeks earlier. It was James' house. He could do what he wanted. But still ...

"All right," he sighed. No use getting emotional about it. What was the point? "How long is he staying?"

"I don't know. That's the thing. He doesn't even know. Rick, he doesn't even have any cash to get himself a hotel room. Otherwise …"

"I understand," Rick lied. "I get it." He was silent for a moment. Ballser bellowed something else at James.

"Hold the fuck on!" James yelled back, not holding the phone far enough from his mouth. "I've got to go, Rick. I'm sorry."

"James," Rick said. "What about us? How are we going to do this?" He had a feeling he already knew the answer and held his breath for it. Hope was fading.

"Rick," came the quiet, sad answer. "There's no way. Not around him."

"Well, that's really cowardly for a military man, isn't it?"

"You don't understand."

"I understand enough."

"Rick. Wait! Listen, we can pick this up again when he leaves …"

"No, James," Rick said. If he had the tears left, this was where he would have sniffed one back. "You can't do me like that. I'm not a side of beef you can put in the refrigerator to be warmed up later when it suits you better."

"That's not what I meant, and you know it!" His voice was actually rising a little.

"Goodbye, James." He hung up and threw the phone across the room tiredly.

They were all the same, every guy he had ever dated. They lied. None of them ever truly loved him. And James was even worse than Coby. At least Coby never pretended to be anything but a cheat. He had never done anything even remotely romantic for Rick. Theirs was a symbiotic relationship, merely companionship for sex. With James, though, Rick thought there was something. James had given him flowers, prepared candle-lit dinners, danced with him cheek-to-cheek, and serenaded him with the guitar. Sex was just a fabulous bonus.

But James was just like Coby when push came to shove. Their fears were greater than their convictions and needs, both of them. Rick would never again go through what he had been through with Coby. No matter how genuine James seemed.

CHAPTER 10

Patrick had done everything he could to stay away from his home, and, most notably, Nanna. A week had passed since Sandy had told him his grandmother had been snooping around Cassie's house. It was very unfortunate for him that the day she chose to go sleuthing was the same day he was watching gay porn in the TV room.

Why hadn't she told his mother yet? What was she waiting for? The questions gnawed at him like that damn tie his mother made him wear around his neck almost every day as a child.

While he waited for Nanna to make her move, he did what Melinda thought he was doing all along. He woke every morning, changed into his uniform of a polo and khakis (which he would wear all day), clean the pool, and do anything else Cassie needed done around the house. Anytime Cassie would request that he slow down and take a rest, he would make up some excuse to continue. She suspected something was amiss, but didn't question him further. If he was ever tempted to have a dip in the pool or just watch movies with Vera and Cassie, he would remember his grandmother's ever-present leer.

The same leer followed him out the front door as he headed to Cassie's the morning of the porn party.

"Have fun," she hissed.

Were turtles supposed to hiss?

He shuddered and walked outside. Her eyes burned into him as she watched from the window holding her "Jesus is Coming-Are You Ready?" mug.

He smiled wickedly at himself. He was on his way to an evening of gay porn, and it was Jesus who was coming? Good for Jesus.

He would help Cassie, Vera, and Becky get ready for the party. That was his job, after all. That's why he was overpaid the big bucks. But he would also remember to keep an eye on every window. Maybe he would even enlist Justin and Sandy to help him. It shouldn't be that hard.

"Patrick, honey!" Vera exclaimed, as Patrick walked into the pool area through the back gate. "Are we ready to watch some good porn, sweets?"

Terrence had spent all morning on the sofa in a t-shirt and plaid pajama bottoms, flipping through the myriad of channels on the 70-inch screen that Cliff had given David as an anniversary gift. He watched cooking shows while he ate breakfast. This was always a habit of his that made him jealous of what was being made, not to mention a little disappointed with his own cold cereal or bran muffin. Eventually, he settled on a movie channel and *Tea with Mussolini*.

"Cher, Lilly Tomlin, *and* Maggie Smith?" he said to himself. "Yes!"

He wondered if Christian would share his taste in film. It was a subject they had barely touched. He knew he was a fan of Monty Python, but what kid at that age wasn't?

It wasn't long, though, before the film was interrupted by the sound of loud music emanating from Rick's room.

"Every morning!" Terrence exclaimed under breath, as he threw his head back and stared at the ceiling in exasperation.

Every day since James had ended things (or had Rick done that?). Rick played nothing but loud, sappy music to be heard. He hardly came out of the room at all. Terrence imagined him curled up in the fetal position on his bed, clutching a picture of James, while he sobbed and listened to Joan Baez. That's how Terrence would have dealt with the situation, except he would have added a bottle of gin and replaced Joan Baez with Morrissey. Then he would have posted rumors about the asshole who did him wrong all over the internet and through the local club system.

Terrence rose from his comfortable position and knocked on Rick's door. He had to knock again over the stereo. "Ricky!" he yelled.

Joan's voice was the only answer.

"Rick, you can't go on like this forever," Terrence hollered. "Things will change, sugar. Why don't you open the door? We can talk about it. I'll take you out to eat."

Still, no response.

"What's going on?" David asked, walking into the room in his Ginch Gonch boxer briefs. "Is he still locked in there?"

"Yeah. I can't get him out," Terrence answered. "And if I have to hear 'Diamonds & Rust' one more time, I'm going to break down this fucking door."

"Ricky!" David shouted, with more force than Terrence could summon. He pounded on the door, shaking the wall. "Enough is enough. Get out of there!"

"Leave me the fuck alone!" Rick finally shouted from inside.

"You'll meet someone else. I promise," David said.

"You don't get it." Rick sounded beaten. "There's no way you could."

"What's that supposed to mean?" Terrence asked David.

"Why don't you come out of there?" David tried again. "Cassie's porn party is today. That'll be fun. You might meet someone there." He waited for an answer. "Rick?"

"I'm not going!" Rick shouted. "Fuck off!"

"I'll give him a few more days," David explained to Terrence. "But if he doesn't get out of that funk soon, we're busting that door open. The bitch needs an intervention."

"He must be really stuck on James. I've never seen Rick show this much emotion."

"Maybe if he showed his emotions more often he wouldn't be such a damn mess." David walked away, visibly concerned and upset, his hands on his hips.

Terrence continued to speak outside the door, but Rick wasn't listening. He couldn't have heard anything even if he tried. Terrence had a softer voice than David. There was no way he could out-voice Joan Baez on stereo.

He appreciated their concern. Really, he did. But they would never truly understand how he felt, how every rejection seared into him like acid until the nerves were nearly deadened. Nearly, but not completely. Dammit, he still had feeling!

He was damaged, an incomplete person. It was possible that no man would ever love him. He was certain Coby never had, and though James seemed like the real deal, that had fallen apart as well. But he had learned from past hurts. Eventually, sighs, shrugs, and dead stares replaced tears and sobs.

He walked to the antique dressing mirror across the room. His face was drawn with self-doubt and regret. He removed the eye patch slowly. It was as if he felt pain while removing it. He cringed at the thought of what lay under it, hidden away. That idea hurt more than the loss of the eye itself.

He forced himself to look at the dark, sunken flesh. Incomplete, he thought again. Damaged. James had called it a battle scar, and that had helped. It had meant something. Rick had even managed to stop hiding his patch with his hand. He had felt so comfortable with James. So normal.

But that was all gone. It would never come back.

By six in the evening, Cassie Bloom's gay porn spectacular was well underway. She was a firm believer in squeezing as much fun into as much time as possible. Being fashionably late was for the insecure and the boring.

The guests arrived in excited droves. They were a broad array of women from the neighborhood, young couples with whom Cassie was acquainted with and the young, gay men she adored. A few single, straight men came along as well. A party was a party, after all, and Cassie's parties featured great food, free alcohol, and lots of single, horny women. The house was crowded by eight. A random gay flick played in each room of the ground floor, though the main show was, of course, in the TV room.

Cassie even had a large screen set out back by the pool, because, sooner or later, that's where the party would end up. The pool was always a big draw. She and Patrick had spent a large part of the day getting the 'faerie' lights strung up and working correctly. The rest of the day they spent blowing up the penis-shaped balloons.

Inside, people mingled, drank, and laughed. The food adhered to the theme of the night as well. Everything was a phallus, from the cupcakes to the crab cakes.

There were heathen games as well, and prizes to make each participant's sex life blister with excitement. A few impatient revelers even ran off to dark corners of the house after their wins. Body creams, dildos, copies of the most scintillating new gay porn releases, and harnesses, even a few whips, made it into the hands of the guests. The house was replete with laughter.

"What's this?" asked a younger woman whom Cassie had met recently. She held aloft an object that had just been bestowed on her after winning a game. She was innocent, Cassie knew, but, oh, the pleasures she could open for herself if she gave up certain restrictions of the mind.

"That's a cock ring, honey," answered Ruth, one of the oldest inhabitants of Jasper Lane. "You put it on his willie," she explained, pointing to the young woman's husband.

His face turned beat red. They both stared at the cock ring, then back at the old woman, and began to laugh along with everyone else.

"Next game," Cassie called out. "Any suggestions?" She stood beside the TV as the game's participants were seated before her, some on the sofa, some on the floor, and some standing.

"I've got one," David replied, as he sat on the floor between Cliff's legs. "How many times will the guy in the next scene say 'Oh yeah! Fuck me'?"

Everyone laughed.

"Good one," Cassie said. "Everyone write your answer down on the sheet."

The guests who were playing did as asked, and watched the next scene unfold. A butch cop was mopping the floor with a new recruit, literally. The recruit seemed to be in ecstasy.

"He's really not that good," Cliff interjected. "The cop, I mean."

David hushed him as the count began.

"Oh yeah! Fuck me!"

"Oh yeah! Fuck me!"

"Oh yeah! Fuck me!"

"Oh! Fuck, yeah!"

"That one doesn't count," Cassie said.

All told, and groaned, there were seven such exclamations of exaltation.

"That's some good acting," Cliff said.

"All right. Who had seven?" Cassie asked.

Patrick and Sandy raised their hands.

"Way to go, Patrick!" Vera congratulated.

"I never win," Terrence moaned on the sofa, as Becky gave him a comforting hug.

Cassie handed out the prizes. Patrick regarded his with complete confusion. It was red and looked like a thin, crooked dildo.

"What is this?" he asked, viewing it from different angles.

"It's a prostate tickler," Justin told him. "You put it up your bum."

"Really?" Patrick smiled in disbelief.

"Trust me," Justin said. "It's a good time, even for a straight kid like you."

Sandy had an easier time with her prize, though her expression was just as comical.

"What am I supposed to do with this?" She giggled, as she held the nine inch dildo with life-like scrotum in her hands. "I've got all the dick I need from my husband, thank you."

David fidgeted nervously. Cliff massaged his shoulders.

"Well, look," Vera said, taking the phallus from her. "It ejaculates. You squeeze the balls while submerging the head in a liquid, and then squeeze them again to release." She demonstrated how it worked by dipping the dildo into Sandy's drink. As she squeezed the bulbous faux testes, Sandy's drink suddenly diminished in volume.

"I dare you to take a shot," Vera said, holding the dildo up to Sandy.

"No way!" Sandy laughed, her eyes wide.

"I'll give you twenty dollars," Vera pressured.

"I'll do it!" Ruth exclaimed, as she grabbed the fake dong from Vera. "Hell, it's twenty bucks!" She whipped her head back, and squeezed hard on the balls, getting every last bit of alcohol from the rubber scrotum. The group went up in a roar of laughter.

"This was my very first scene!" Cliff said, drawing everyone's attention back to the screen.

The group watched as Cliff, dressed in a cop's uniform, walked into a jail cell to interrogate a prisoner. The tables were soon turned, however, as the prisoner and a fellow cop had Cliff stripped and bent over the bed, his muscular butt raised high in the air.

"And they go to town," David said, clearly having seen the film before.

"Shhh! Don't ruin it for us," Becky teased.

Both cop and prisoner took turns riding the poor cop. Then, as if that weren't enough, every other cop and prisoner in the place-extraordinarily good-looking, all of them-had their way with Cliff's ass.

"That was my first gang bang," Cliff explained. "I won an award for that."

"And so you should have," Cassie said. "That's fucking hot, honey!"

"And it's all mine," David said, as he leaned back for a kiss.

Cassie leered at him playfully. "Maybe, but I paid for a stripper tonight. Cliff?"

"It's your money," he said, as he rose.

"Focus on the ass," Becky winked. "That's the moneymaker."

"Don't tell me how to do my job," he fussed back with a grin.

The gamers cheered him on as he began stripping to the music from his very first porn.

As soon as Sandy had left for Cassie Bloom's party, Steve popped the DVD in the player. He was like a football coach, dissecting his own plays, remarking to himself what worked and what didn't, and what could be done better.

He still couldn't find the DVD he had hidden in the basket with the linens and table blankets. In fact, the entire basket had disappeared when he finally remembered it. Luckily, another film had arrived just a few days later.

He hadn't been interested in seeing himself being screwed by another man, but then Evan had said that viewing his last performance might help him be better in the future. And since this was his career for the time being, he would treat it like any other gig he ever had. Being the constant professional and perfectionist, he would be the best darned gay-for-pay actor in the business. He was even starting to get the moaning and groaning down pat. The gay boys seemed to really like it. His new noisy love-making trickled into the bedroom with Sandy as well. She very much appreciated his new style. It excited her when he moaned dirty words into her ears, and was a little rougher than before.

He watched the scene where Evan came all over his stomach. Steve's own sexual exclamations were the star of the scene, though, as he shot his load.

"Not bad," Steve admitted.

But it could be better, he thought. He needed to show the ass more. Hoist it higher in the air. That was what Gabriel wanted.

Steve was becoming quite the sensation at the studio, and whispers of greatness were being echoed down the corridors of gay-video vaults. He was being mentioned in the same breath as Caesar. Admittedly, Steve had no idea who that was, but from the sound of him he was an impressive sex star.

Now, Gabriel had just signed Steve to a three-picture deal, and he was to be the star of all of them. A title had yet to be decided for the trilogy, but the subject matter itself was Gabriel's idea. Steve was to play a football player riding fame and all his ballplayer buddies along the way.

It was going to make him a lot of money.

Then, too, there were the internet sessions. Gabriel had set up a webcam at the studio, and, for a few hours every week, Steve would pose and jack off for an enraptured audience. His shows were drawing huge numbers and many devoted fans.

To keep the money pouring in, of course, he needed to keep in shape. His regular routine with David every night was beefed up even more with some advice from Cliff. Soon Steve was looking even buffer than before.

"But never shave," Gabriel advised. "Your fans love the hair."

That was good to hear. Steve was uncomfortable with the idea of shaving his body hair in the first place. Sandy liked it, and what would she think if he suddenly shaved? At the very least, she would think he had another woman.

Steve paused the film as another couple of straight guys appeared on the screen. No need to watch them.

"I'm doing it for her," he whispered. "It's all for her and the baby. We need the money."

And it was all true. Yet the misery he felt at not being able to explain to Sandy exactly what it was he did was unbearable. His guilt tore him up inside.

"Patrick!" Cassie laughed. "Get down from there! You're going to hurt yourself."

He only smiled at her, acknowledging that he had indeed heard her above the screams of adoration as he danced with Cliff on the dining room table, an old mahogany thing that had belonged to Cassie's mother-in-law. He strutted about in his underwear to a Donna Summers record, shaking his butt at the onlookers. Cliff let him have the moment. He enjoyed sharing the stage with the energetic straight kid.

"Hey now!" David kidded, as Patrick grinded into Cliff's rear.

Patrick wasn't drunk. Not a sip all evening. Cassie wouldn't allow it. She had set some rules for him. His energy stemmed from the sheer satisfaction of having a good time. It was a rare occurrence for him.

"That table is going to collapse any minute," Vera said to Cassie.

"Eh," Cassie shrugged. "Good riddance to bad memories."

"Who knew Frank and Melinda Gold could create someone like him?" Terrence observed.

The music was coming to an end, but the crowd that had assembled cheered for more. Ruth, who was extremely intoxicated, wanted to climb on the table with the guys as well, but was talked out of it by Vera.

"Honey, if that table breaks," Vera explained, "all that's going to be left of you when Cliff is pulled up off you will be a wrinkly ol' bag of bones."

"Then I'll die a happy gal!" the old woman replied.

"But we still need you here, honey." And in the end, Vera won out.

Justin and Sandy stood near the back of the crowd, laughing at the spectacle happening before their eyes. Sandy suddenly jabbed Justin in the arm, and pointed to a nearby window. As Justin looked, he caught the unmistakable flash of a camera, the old kind that journalists from the mid-twentieth century used.

Immediately, Justin left Sandy's side and raced out the door, passing other guests who were not watching the striptease. On the porch, he saw a limping form struggling to hurry away. Night had descended, and it was difficult to see more than a silhouette.

"Did anybody see an old lady with a camera?" he asked some guests assembled on the porch.

They all regarded the question with indifference and replied in the negative.

He walked back in to Sandy's side. "I think it was her," he said. "No one saw for certain, though."

"Well, if they had gotten a good look at her they would know," Sandy responded. "The woman is hideous."

"Do you think she got a picture?"

"It doesn't matter if she did or not. Patrick's in for it, I'm afraid. She'll be sure to squeal on him to Melinda."

They watched as Patrick was finally coaxed down from the table and Cassie shoved his clothes into his arms.

"I think you might have just found something to get you through college," she joked.

"Assuming I ever go," he said, slipping his shirt back on.

"You will."

Patrick glanced up and saw Justin and Sandy motioning at him.

"I'll be right back," he said.

He knew what they were going to say even before he heard the words from Justin's mouth. He knew he had been careless, and his mother would soon find out, if she hadn't already, about his secret life.

"Patrick. I'm sorry," Justin said.

It was the umpteenth call that week. At first, James was sure Rick just needed time to adjust. That he would come around and they might indeed be able to pick up where things had left off before Ballser intruded. He realized soon, though, that was not going to happen. Rick had changed his cell phone number, and Terrence would deflect him when he tried to call the landline at David's house.

"He's not here," he had said at first, rather gruffly ... well, as gruffly as Terrence could.

But soon he became more truthful. "Rick doesn't want to talk to you, James. You broke his heart, you asshole! How's that feel, bitch? Huh? You broke his heart."

Those words gauged deeper than any shrapnel ever could.

"Could you at least give him a message?" James pleaded, licking his dry lips.

"Maybe," Terrence replied shortly.

James could just imagine him, standing there with a hand on his hip, tapping his foot irritably, jaw clenched and eyebrow raised.

"Just ... just tell him I'm sorry."

"Oh, you can do better than that!" Terrence snorted, as he hung up the phone.

Once James realized that none of his messages over the phone would do any good, he tried to sneak over to see Rick while Ballser was still sleeping off a hangover. It was only a few houses down, but with a homophobic army dick following him most of the time like a starved kitten, it was a precarious venture.

"You get right now!" Terrence snapped, before James even had the chance to knock on the door. He stood behind the screen with the face of an angry parent.

"I just want to talk with him," James said. "Let me talk to him."

"There's nothing you can say. Trust me."

"I want to apologize," James insisted.

"Are you going to take him back? Are you through playing mother to that army chum? 'Cause that's the only way I'm letting you in, bitch."

"It's not that easy to explain. I can't ... what Rick and I have has to be kept ..."

"Don't you even say 'on the down low'! That's such a ridiculous idea. Rick's been through enough shit in his life. He doesn't need that. He's a real man. He wears his scars on the outside. Just go back to your hetero life mate." There he made a flitting gesture with his fingers.

"Fuck you. I'm going to stay right here," James responded, defiantly.

"I'll call the cop, bitch," Terrence threatened. "I dated a fella in their ranks. We're still on great terms. He'd be more than happy to come down here and bust your ass."

James stared at him, a mix of pleading and anger in his eyes.

"I said get!" Terrence ordered again.

And that was it. James was back in his big, inherited house filled with nothing but a dead man's memories and a snoring blockhead in one of the many rooms.

James knew Rick's cell number was void, yet he couldn't help but try it once more. Still nothing. He threw his phone on the sofa, and looked out the window onto the night-time street. He imagined Rick was most likely at Cassie's party, but then reevaluated that assertion. If Rick was as upset as Terrence was portraying, there would be no way he would be in the mood for a party. In truth, James wasn't much in the mood for one either. He had been invited, but ... he couldn't show his face there. Not now.

He flopped onto the sofa, burying his face in his hands. He had broken Rick's heart, and that was more than he could bear. He couldn't ever remember caring as deeply about someone else's feelings before.

"Rick," he whispered.

"Jimmy!" Ballser shouted, making his way into the room with a cold beer in his hand. "There's a big party or somethin' going on at the end of the street. What do you say we crash it?"

"No, man," James replied. "It's not your-our thing." He stood again, pushing up with his hands on his knees, as if he needed the help standing.

"Why not? It's a party, man."

"It's for the ladies … mostly," James said, trying to tactfully answer.

"I dig bachelorette parties. Let's go." He slapped James on the back. "Lots of horny chicks, you know?"

"It's a gay porn party!" James snapped. "Okay? You wouldn't like it."

"A gay porn party?" Ballser repeated. "What the hell? You mean there's a bunch of gals sittin' around watching some homos fucking each other?"

James sighed with an expression of utter annoyance. "Ballser," he said. "When did you say you were leaving?"

Sandy had moved onto the pool area. The night air was humid with a slight breeze. She sipped her Day at the Beach leisurely. If it were a smaller party, just close friends, Cassie would have broken out the crystal stemware. But for a party such as this, where there were sure to be some fumbles and falls, the good stuff was kept behind closed cupboard doors. Already the dining room table had collapsed as Ruth climbed on it to dance to "Sex Bomb." Luckily, David had been there to catch her as she fell. She gave him a big, wet kiss for his efforts.

Sandy examined her surroundings. There were a few couples scattered here and there. Not nearly as many as she thought would be out by this time. The party on the inside had been very entertaining, though. The young couple who had won the cock ring earlier in the night made out relentlessly in Cassie's Jacuzzi. Sandy turned away quickly, not interested in being a voyeur.

From inside the house, she heard a familiar voice. She smiled as she hurried back.

"Steve! You're here!" she shouted as she rushed into a room that had suddenly gone hushed.

A hallway of faces on all sides stared at her with expectant looks.

"What?" she asked. "What is it? Where's Steve? I heard his voice …"

And then she saw him. He was indeed at the party, but not in person. Instead, he was magnified on the screen, being fucked by another man, moaning as he did with her in bed. She dropped her drink to the carpet and nearly lost her balance.

"Sandy?" David came forward. "Sandy, breathe." He took hold of her hand.

"Turn it off," Cassie whispered to Becky.

Sandy walked near the TV and picked up the DVD case. Her husband's handsome face stared at her from the cover.

"Did you know about this?" she asked David.

He stared at her for a moment, then nodded.

"He did it for you and the baby!" he shouted as she ran out the door. A host of rapt eyes followed her as her. Her anger mounted with each long stride home.

Steve had finished observing and critiquing his performances. All in all, it looked good, but there was always room for improvement.

He was brushing his teeth when he heard the door slam down stairs. That was odd. He had never known Sandy to slam anything.

"Baby," he called. "Is that you?"

He spit into the sink, dried his mouth with a towel, and then descended the stairs. Sandy stood by the large living-room window. Her back was to him.

"Hey, sweetie," he said, coming near to embrace her. "I thought you'd stay later. I was going to wait up for you on the porch."

As he touched her, she reeled around, hitting him with something hard and plastic. The edge of it scratched him on the forearm.

"What is this?" she screamed. "What the hell is this?"

"What? Baby, what's wrong?" He staggered backward. The scratch was bleeding.

"This!" she shouted, showing him the DVD case. "They were watching it at the party. Everyone in the neighborhood! They all saw you being ... screwed by that man!"

"That's where it went," he whispered to himself, connecting the dots. "I'm sorry. Sandy, I'm sorry!"

"You're sorry?" she screeched. "You're sorry?"

"I did it for you," he defended. "We needed the money. That's what got me through it."

"Shut up! I don't want to hear the excuses." She was crying, bawling. She began hitting him with the DVD case again, as he shielded himself with his arms and backed toward the door.

"Get out! Get out of our house! I never want to see you again!"

"Sandy, you don't mean that. Please!" He was sobbing as he was forced onto the porch.

Sandy threw the case at him, and slammed the door.

"Sandy! Sandy, please!" he bellowed through tears.

His voice was met by glass and wood. Sandy had sunk to the floor, sobbing with her back against the door.

CHAPTER 11

It should have been a lovely morning.

David opened his eyes as gentle ribbons of sunshine streamed in across the bed where he lay naked, wrapped in his expensive, white, cotton sheets. Cliff lay next to him, still asleep, his chest heaving and his eyes twitching to some dream or fantasy. One huge, muscular thigh lay uncovered. The birds sang outside on the limbs of the trees, and a soft breeze wafted in from the screen window.

Yes, it could have been a perfect morning. He could have just lain there, snuggling into Cliff's chest and arms as soon as he stirred.

Even though Steve moved in after Sandy had kicked him out of the house, things were still not too loud. One would think there would be a constant orchestra of noise with four, sometimes five, guys living in the same house. But Steve was gone in the mornings most of the time, either filming (he still had a contract) or apologizing to Sandy. Rick was as quiet as ever, and Terrence was usually too hung over to stand any noises at all.

But that was not the case this morning.

The tranquility of the late summer morning was destroyed by a loud racket downstairs. Terrence screamed at the top of his lungs.

David stumbled out of bed. He didn't worry about waking Cliff. That was an impossibility. Cliff could have slept right through the opening ceremonies of the Olympics even if he were in the very center of it. David didn't bother putting any clothes on, but went down the stairs, angry and loud.

"What the hell is going on?" he yelled.

Terrence was chasing Rick, who carried a cardboard box out the door.

"He's leaving!" Terrence explained. "He's moving out because of James!"

"What?" David asked at the bottom of the stairs. He rubbed his eyes and walked to the door.

Sure enough, Rick had loaded his CDs into his little blue car.

"We can't let him get his clothes!" Terrence said. "I'm going to lock him out of the room!" And off he hurried, shutting himself in Rick's room and locking it.

As Rick came back from the car, David tried to reason. "Ricky, come on," he said. "Just calm down."

"I'm not worked up," Rick replied. "I am calm. I've just made a decision. It's been two weeks, David. He's not coming back to me, so I'm moving on." He passed David and headed to his room.

"Moving on means moving out?"

"He's just a few houses down," Rick said. "It's very awkward." He stood at the door. "Terrence, let me in!"

"No!" Terrence shouted. "I'm not going to let you leave!"

"How about we talk about this?" David pleaded.

Rick walked to the front door again. "Nothing to talk about," he said. He slammed the door behind him, and headed around to the back of the house.

David, aware that his nudity might offend some of the neighbors, grabbed a throw that Terrence had hung on the wall and draped it around himself, following Rick outside.

"I appreciate everything you guys have done for me. I mean that," Rick said. "But I can't do this again."

"Of course not," David agreed, as they came to the back garden. "But … Rick, wait!"

Rick waited at the garden door to his room. Terrence, having forgotten to pay any heed to that door, screamed with surprise at seeing them there. He had pulled the chest of drawers against the other door, but hadn't thought to block the garden door. He raced towards it, but Rick opened the door before Terrence could reach it.

"Just let me to talk with James," David said. "Let me talk to him. Let me see what's really going through his head."

Rick searched his friend's eyes.

"Come on, Ricky. A few more days won't hurt. If things can't get figured out, I promise, neither of us will get in your way if you still want to leave. We love you, Ricky."

"Is that my throw?" Terrence interrupted, staring at David in horror through the screen door.

David ignored him. "Ricky?"

"Okay," Rick agreed with a sigh. "You talk to him. But I don't want to look at the coward."

He stepped into his room, past Terrence. David pulled Terrence out and they left him alone.

"Are you going to talk to Army Guy now?" Terrence asked as they made their way back around front.

"As soon as I can get Cliff up and moving."

"Thank goodness! I have to go pick up Christian from the airport. Even if I had managed to stop Rick from leaving, the little bitch would have escaped while I was gone."

"Oh, yeah! The little one is coming in today. Are you excited?"

"Scared shitless," Terrence admitted.

"It'll be fine."

"I know," Terrence said with a smile. "Hey, David?"

"What?"

"Take off my throw!" Terrence screamed, as he ripped the wall-hanging from David's body, leaving him naked and exposed. "This thing costs more than this entire house, bitch!" he said, as he folded it in his arms and marched inside.

Every morning for a week Steve had been back on his porch, waiting for Sandy to emerge. Every morning he held a bouquet of flowers and apologized profusely, and every morning she would take the flowers from him without saying a word and shut the door again. He assumed she threw them out or circumcised the blooms from the stems. Then he would leave for the studio, but his mind was distracted. Gabriel could ascertain that much.

"Where are you?" Gabriel had asked as Steve spaced out in the middle of a solo scene in his much-anticipated football trilogy.

"I'm sorry, Gabriel."

"What's wrong, Steve?"

The director, a pot-bellied man with bad skin, yelled "Cut!"

Gabriel pulled Steve aside.

"After this is over … after the filming for the trilogy is done, I'm going to have to quit," Steve said.

"We can talk about it later," Gabriel responded with a comforting pat on the shoulder.

"No, Gabriel. It's got to be over."

"You never told the wife, huh?"

Steve shook his head and stared at the floor. "I've fucked everything up."

"Go home," Gabriel said. "We'll finish this later."

It was good that he actually had some type of home to return to. David offered a temporary bed at his place. It saved him from getting a motel room, a move that surely would have made him feel like the stereotypical defunct husband.

And, yes, he realized now it was cheating. It was sex with another person, after all. Why had he convinced himself that just because it was with a man, someone to whom he was in no way truly attracted, that it wasn't truly stepping out on Sandy?

If he were a lesser man he might have searched for someone to blame for his predicament. If he hadn't been fired, if they hadn't chosen to live in such an expensive house, if David hadn't brought the notion of the gay-for-pay industry to his attention … but that was not Steve's style. He was a strong man who made his own decisions, and he always took responsibility for the outcomes of those decisions.

There was no way the firm could stay afloat any longer.

And they lived in the house on Jasper Lane because they had earned it, saved hard for it.

And David was the best friend Steve had ever had, and was only concerned about his and Sandy's well-being. Blaming him for anything was avoiding real issues.

He stood on their porch with a bouquet of roses again. Again, Sandy opened the door, but this time she stared at him for a minute. His eyes could not hold hers, and he looked away. She took the roses from him and gestured him into the house. He followed submissively.

He sat at the kitchen table as she fixed them both coffee. The wall clock ticked. The air conditioner hummed. The silence between them was like a stretched rubber band, ready to snap. He wanted to say something, but there were no words that would be worthy. All of his apologizing was useless. He would have liked to have shown her how sorry he was, but she might only recoil.

What was she thinking? What did she think of him? Did she even love him any more?

"The baby's room is coming along nicely," she finally said.

"Uh, great." He swallowed his anxiety with the hot coffee. Too hot. She liked it that way, but it burned his mouth.

"The painters came earlier this week. I let them in, but I didn't hang around to watch."

"You trust them?"

"Trust? You want to talk about trust? No. Let's not talk about trust."

He looked down ashamedly at the mug. Steam rose from it in vaporous lines of beauty.

"I'm sorry," she said more softly. "I know you did it for us. I know all that money goes to our future, our happiness. It's just a twisted way to get there, don't you think?"

"I should have told you. I should have run the idea by you …"

"Well, you know what I would have said. That's why you didn't."

Tick tock, goes the clock.

"It's just, I love you so much. I love the baby already, so much."

She hushed him with her expression. "No. You don't get to explain it away like that. We'll work through it, maybe with a therapist, but there will be no explaining it away." She paused to take a drink. "I'm not happy about it. The idea that the baby's room is being paid for by money you made getting screwed on film … The baby will never find out about it."

"I've already told the studio head that I'm through after my contract is up. I can't get out before then. They'll take everything we have. I'll get a real job. I swear it."

"Did you enjoy it?" she asked, staring intently into his eyes. She wanted nothing but truth.

"The sex? Of course not. I've never been attracted to men. You know that."

"I don't know what I know," she mumbled. "And neither do you. To tell you the truth, I don't know if the fact that it didn't mean anything makes it better or worse."

Steve was trembling. He could have burst into a billion particles right there. "It was acting. That's all."

The room was frozen in dramatic anticipation.

"Give me another week," Sandy said. "Then you can come home. We'll need to work on things before we sleep in the same bed again, though. I don't know if it will ever be the same again."

Patrick laid out a lounge chair in his own back yard. The plastic was hard and uncomfortable. It would leave patterns of his resting masochism. After hearing from Justin and Sandy that there had been a flash in the window while he was dancing with Cliff on the table, he knew without a doubt that Nanna had the evidence to prove her point to Melinda. Patrick told Cassie he would need to quit, and then walked back home.

Nanna hadn't said anything right away. She seemed to revel in his anxious trudging around her. She had him. She had won.

It was in the kitchen the following evening that Patrick finally came free with it. He walked in and made his proclamation of independence.

"I'm not going to let you do this to me, you old bitch!" he said, as he glared at Nanna from the doorway. There had been no real cause for it. Neither Nanna nor Melinda was even conversing.

"Patrick!" his mother exclaimed. She stopped her mincing and stared at him in shock.

And then he told her. Nanna might never have said anything. She could have just used the photo to get whatever she wanted as leverage. But Patrick wanted his downfall to be on his terms. Indeed, a look of disappointment swept over Nanna's face.

She limped to her room and came back with the picture anyway. Patrick was grinding on the large bodybuilder who occasionally stayed with the boys down the street.

"Patrick!" Melinda again gasped in disbelief. She grabbed the photo with dismay.

His fantasy escape from his family was put to an end. Nanna saw to that. Patrick had made a lot of money working for Cassie, but not nearly enough to go out on his own. He knew very little of the world, of its costs. He had been sheltered, perhaps too long, by a stringent mother and a bitter, suffocating grandmother.

"Wait until your father hears about this!" Melinda cried.

"He might hear, but he'll never listen, Mom," Patrick shot back.

"What do you mean by that, young man?"

"When's the last time you had an actual conversation with him? When's the last time he showed you or me anything but indifference?"

Now he lay on the chair thinking of the things he might have done had he gotten away. He wanted to smash every window he could find. Nanna watched him from the sliding glass door, eating up his misery like pudding.

He glanced at her, flipping her off. She gave him "the eye" before backing away slowly, like a monster into dark shadows.

"Stay away from my son!" Melinda said stalwartly as she stood on Cassie's porch. Her hands were clenched tight. "I don't want him over here any more. Do you understand?"

It had taken her the whole week to gather the courage to march down the street to the Bloom house. She had once wanted Cassie to be her friend. She thought that they were becoming very close already. But now she wondered how she could have ever possessed the desire to start a friendship with her. Nanna was right. Cassie Bloom was nothing but a harlot and a murderess.

"He quit last week," Cassie responded. Her face was emotionless, tired. She leaned against the door for support, her arms folded.

"Good," Melinda said. She stood puffed up and proud, so sure she was in the right.

"Don't look at me with that condescending expression, Melinda. I'm fucking tired of it. Everyone is. You're no better than the rest of us. We're all just trying to get by."

"I'm better than this!" Melinda pulled out the photo, shoving it in Cassie's face.

"How did you get this?" Cassie inquired. "Have you been spying on my house? That's an invasion of privacy. I should call the police."

Melinda withdrew the photo, her face slackened with a modicum of fear.

"Stay away from my son, Cassie. You'll understand if I don't invite you over for coffee any more." She turned abruptly and began walking away, her heels clicking like a chiding tongue.

"You're smothering him," Cassie said loudly. "He's going to hate you for it. He might already. For his sake, and yours, give him some air."

"I know my own son!" Melinda yelled back. "Don't you think I know my son? Don't you think any good mother would know her own son?" She almost tripped as she began walking faster down the sidewalk.

Cassie closed the door gently and stood for a moment with her forehead against the doorframe. Melinda was making a mistake by keeping such a tight hold over her son, but what could she do about it? Patrick wasn't her son. As much as he reminded her of Jason, they were not one and the same.

"Don't you think any good mother would know her own son?" she repeated quietly.

As she walked to the living room, she heard Jason's voice echo through the house.

"You killed him! I know you killed him! One day I'll prove it! I never want to see you again!"

And while his accusation was untrue, she had indeed wanted to kill Jackson. She could have and would never have felt the worse for it. If only she could tell Jason why. That it was for him. That everything was always for him.

"Holy shit!" Ballser shouted as he opened the door to David and the mountain of muscle that was Cliff. Cliff sported his tiniest tank top and his fiercest expression. His flexing pectoral alone could knock Ballser back a few feet.

Ballser chewed the cereal in his mouth like a cow chewed cud, dipping the spoon into the bowl once more for another heap of Trix.

"Where's James?" David asked, none too politely.

"Who's askin'?" Ballser grunted, spitting out bits of colored cereal.

"Where is he?" David asked again.

Cliff wasn't as gracious. He pushed Ballser out of the way, and they walked in. Ballser spilled milk over the front of his already stained, white t-shirt.

"Hey, ass!" he shouted.

Cliff whirled around and looked at him with frightening intensity. Ballser immediately stiffened, his eyes widening.

"Jimmy!" he hollered. "Yo, Jimmy! There's a monster and his boy here to see you!"

James walked into the room, clearly irritated by the sound of Ballser's voice bouncing off the walls of the old house.

"What is it?" he groaned.

"What's up, James?" David greeted.

James stared at the two of them. His eyes kept returning to the barely clothed torso of Cliff.

"Hey, fellas," he said, a nervous tremor in his voice. "How's Rick?"

"That's why we're here," David said.

"Rick? Who's Rick?" Ballser interrupted. He continued to shovel the cereal into his mouth.

"He was James' boyfriend for a little bit, wasn't he?"

"Boyfriend?" Ballser laughed. He sized up David and Cliff. "So, that's it. You two are fairies. That's what all them muscles are covering for. Sorry but Jimmy ain't no queer!"

"You better shut that yap of yours," Cliff warned.

"Or what? I ain't scared of no fucking pillow biter. I'm an army man. You better back the fuck off."

"Ballser," James warned, "don't be a moron."

But the warning went unheeded and he pushed Cliff's chest. "Faggot!"

In the next instant, Ballser lay unconscious on the wood floor.

"I was a marine," Cliff said with a grin as he stood over his cereal-soaked antagonist. He cracked his knuckles with satisfaction.

"You need to talk to Rick, and soon," David said, turning his attention back to James.

"How can I? He won't answer the phone, and every time I head over there Terrence won't let me in. He threatens to call the cops."

"Terrence does that, huh?" David shook his head, irritated. "That sounds like him."

"I would love to talk to Rick."

"He said you wanted to stall things."

"Yeah. Until Ballser left. He doesn't know I'm gay."

"Does now. So you've got no reason not to stay away from him."

"Oh my God," James said, sitting on the couch. "That's true. You just outed me. He's going to tell everyone."

"Good!" David said, as they turned to leave. "For most things, I find that honesty is truly the best policy, unless, of course, you're trying to cover up a murder."

"How am I going to do this?" James asked.

"You better think of something," Cliff replied. "I don't like to see David unhappy. And if Rick leaves, David's going to be very unhappy, and I'm going to have to kick your ass. Got it?"

They stepped over Ballser's sprawled form on the floor. James sat and stared at his annoying house guest's motionless body.

How was he going to fix this? He wanted to be with Rick, but what about his family? Once Ballser awoke he would certainly tell them. James wondered if his own happiness was worth the shattered dreams of his parents. One man's dreams were another's nightmares.

As Terrence drove, he couldn't help but look over at his passenger-his son-every few seconds. It was unreal. Here was his sixteen-year-old former self, almost exactly. The resemblance was staggering. It made him consider growing his hair back.

Their reunion in the terminal had been a careful, awkward dance. They circled one another like curious animals, only with broad smiles of recognition, before they finally embraced. When Christian called him "Dad", Terrence thought he would break down in very un-masculine tears right there. How could he keep the act up?

"How's Tes-your mother?" Terrence asked, as they sped down the interstate. He was trying so hard to keep the masculine edge to his voice. It was like a future drag queen walking for the first time in stilettos.

"She's great," Christian answered with a strong, sure voice. He hadn't stopped smiling. It was a wondrous, wide grin. Welcoming and profoundly assuring. "She was excited for me to meet you. She thinks you're great."

"Did she … uh, tell you anything about me?" He coughed in nervous anticipation.

"I know that you're gay, if that's what you mean. And it's all good."

"Oh, thank God!" Terrence sighed, letting his true voice come through. "Thank God it's all good!"

"But Mom didn't tell me," Christian added. "I sorta figured it out myself."

"It was the voice, right? Dammit! I worked so hard on it."

"Yeah," Christian chuckled. His eyes looked at Terrence with a kindness that was both heartwarming and a little confusing.

Was this how sons saw their fathers at his age? Was he, at last, the same as any other father in the world? If so, how wonderful! What a fabulous feeling! He should find a lesbian at once and procreate again!

"So, are you seeing anybody?" Christian asked. "You got a fella?" He sipped from a cola.

"What? Do kids ask those kinds of questions of their parents?"

"Sure. You still have sex, right? You're not *that* old. I would just like to know more about what's happening in your life, and since we have the gay thing out in the open, I want to know if there's a fella."

"Not right now," Terrence answered. He was embarrassed even answering the question, but delighted by it as well. He liked the directness with which Christian approached things. "What about you? Do you have a girlfriend?"

"Yeah. Her name is Vanessa. We've been going out for a few months. She wants to meet you. She thinks it's awesome that my dad is gay."

"I'd like to meet her," Terrence said. "So, your mother … she never married?"

"Nah. She dates, but nothing serious. There was this one guy when I was younger, but nothing ever came of it." He paused, changing the subject. "So, this house you live in. Is it old?"

"It's one of the older homes on the street, yes. It was there before the neighborhood was built, as was the house at the very end of the street where Miss Cassie Bloom lives. You'll like her."

"I like old houses," Christian answered.

Terrence smiled. "And antiques? Do you like antiques?"

"Are you kidding? Me and Vanessa head out to the antique malls whenever we can. It's our weekend tradition."

Sandy pulled her long hair back into a ponytail and headed out the front door in a white t-shirt and her college track shorts. She was finally ready to face the eyes of her neighbors-or at least try-after her embarrassment at Cassie's party. She had spent the week, for the most part, behind the safe walls of her own home, but she realized hiding would only prolong her disquiet. She needed to face the questions, the accusations that maybe she wasn't such a good wife. If she were, Steve might never have sought sex elsewhere. She imagined vindictive gossip circulating about her over back fences and summer grill-outs. Stepping out might put an end to that somewhat. So she began speed-walking down Jasper Lane.

She felt their eyes on her, every one of them, but did her best to act as if it didn't weigh on her thoughts at all. She even forced a pleasant half-smile, as if she were thinking of lovely things. Not a concern in the world.

She might have succeeded in her charade of nonchalance if it hadn't been for Becky Ridgeworth and a group of neighborhood women coming toward her, their arms swinging furiously as they power-walked.

Sandy panicked, trying to find a means of escape, some driveway she might disappear into, some open garage. But before she could make her break, Becky called to her.

"Sandy! Sandy! Yoo-hoo!"

"Oh," Sandy said, with a smile that was barely hanging on. "Hi there, Becky. Hello, ladies." She nodded pleasantly to the others as they came up around her. Surrounding her. There was Ruth (damn, that old woman could walk!), the cock-ring girl, and a couple others that Sandy did not know very well.

"You weren't planning on ignoring us, were you?" Becky grinned slyly.

"What? No," Sandy said. "How are you? I was just lost in my own thoughts … thinking … about nothing." She was nervous. Her left eye seemed to be twitching. She was certain someone might think she was having a seizure.

"We're doing well," Becky replied. "I've decided to start an afternoon walking club. Care to join?"

"No, thank you. I've got an elliptical. I just thought I'd take advantage of the nice weather today. Not too hot."

"Sandy," Ruth chimed in with her raspy voice. "We know you've been hiding, darlin', but there ain't no reason to."

"I'm not hiding!" Sandy exclaimed, forcing out a laugh.

"It's okay, hon," Becky consoled. "From what we saw of Steve in that video, you've got every reason to want to keep him to yourself."

"What?" Sandy asked, a little confused.

"That is one fine piece of man meat you've got," Ruth said, licking her wrinkly lips.

"All the girls in the neighborhood are so jealous!" Cock-Ring Girl exclaimed, jumping in her excitement.

"It's true," Becky confirmed. "There's been a run on his videos. I think we might be making you a rich woman."

"Those movies are so hot," one of the other ladies said.

"My sex life has never been better," said another.

Sandy stood there, stunned.

"Anyway," Becky said. "Don't be a stranger. Stop hiding. Your husband's a superstar around here!"

"Maybe he and my Cliffy could do a film together," Ruth suggested. "Whooey! That would be something!"

Sandy was left standing in the middle of the road as the group of power-walking porn watchers chugged on past her.

She wasn't sure what to think. She knew she should be humiliated and angry that her husband was being used for the sexual gratification of others, but, underneath that, she felt a hint of pride.

Steve, her husband, a superstar?

A slight grin came to her lips as she continued on down the street, going from slow walk to light jog.

Maybe she would join the power-walking group after all. She suddenly wanted to hear what else Becky and the other women had to say about Steve's foray into the adult entertainment industry.

Ballser choked just a little on a piece of cereal lodged in his throat as he came to on the hard wood floor. He glanced up to see James standing over him.

"Come on," James said. "Get up." He kicked at the dazed army man.

"What the hell," Ballser groaned, shaking the vertigo from his head. He coughed out an orange *O*.

"Get up," James said again. "You've got to go."

"What?" Ballser asked. His laundry bag sat by the sofa, filled with everything he owned. "Jimmy, what the hell, man!"

"Sorry, Ballser. You've got to go."

"No, I've got to bash some queer heads in!"

"You're not doing anything of the kind. You're going to grab your bag and get the hell out of my house, and you're going to stay out of my life for good. I don't need you. It's harsh, but it needs to be said. You're an obstacle to the rest of my life, man."

James picked up the bag and hoisted it into Ballser's arms.

"But, we're buds, you and me," Ballser said, as James led him to the door.

"We were once. We're not anymore."

"Is this because they said you were gay? Man, I don't believe that. It's only natural they'd want you to be ..."

"Shut the fuck up," James said. They stood outside in the driveway. "You've insulted my friends, you've used me, and, worst of all, you've insulted Rick. I should have spoken up right then."

"Rick? The gardener?" He looked at Steve in shock. "You mean you're a ... fag?"

"Dammit, Ballser," James sighed, as he pulled back and hit the unwanted guest in the jaw. "This is a more enlightened time. Change with the rest of us."

"Fuck!" Ballser exclaimed, holding his face.

A taxi pulled up, and James grabbed Ballser by the shirt. He opened the back door and shoved him in. Ballser fell across the seat. Half his belongings spilled out.

"This is bullshit, Jimmy! There ain't no way you're queer! We've showered together. You've seen my junk!"

"Oh, for God's sake!" James rolled his eyes. "Ballser, do me a favor, will you? Take your oversized ego and tell my parents that their favorite son is gay."

He shut the door, and the cab pulled away.

"This is bullshit, Jimmy!" Ballser yelled from the back seat. "Jimmy!"

James waved happily, sarcastically, as the taxi sped out of sight. He turned and walked back into the house. It was somewhat the worse for wear after Ballser's stay, but James wasn't concerned with that at the moment. He had another wreck to clean up, and barely enough time to do it.

CHAPTER 12

"… And he's smart as a whip!" Terrence exclaimed, completing the list of great accomplishments, deeds, and attributes of his son, Christian. "Much smarter than me. Smarter than anyone I ever knew. He's going places! He's definitely going to change things. He's already thinking of college, and then law school."

He paused and took a bite of his bagel. David waited patiently for him to continue as they both sat in the morning kitchen in their shorts, t-shirts, and sandals. Terrence could hardly keep his enthusiasm at bay while he chewed. He had been up all night talking with his son, and while Christian had eventually dozed off, Terrence remained on a strange high. It was a high more pleasant and rewarding than any drug or alcohol with which he had ever experimented.

"He says he wants to be an attorney, David! And not just any old ambulance-chasing money-whore. No, *my son* wants to do something for society. He's going to be a civil rights lawyer. Can you believe it? He'd be fighting for us!"

"Quite a kid you've got there," David said.

"Don't I know it," Terrence agreed. "He came from me, David. *From me!*"

"Now it just seems silly that you were so nervous about meeting him, doesn't it?"

Terrence rolled his eyes. "Yes, David, you were right. I know that's what you want to hear. There was no reason for me to freak out. And for once, I'm very happy you were right."

"Thank you," David chimed as he took a drink of his protein shake. "So, what's on tap for father and son today?"

"We're going antique shopping."

"You're not! Terry, he's a kid. Why would you want to take him to an old, dusty place that reeks of old age and decline?"

"It was his idea. Apparently, he's quite the son of his father." Terrence had the look of one-upmanship that was rarely seen on his face.

"Okay," David said. "Now it's your turn. Go ahead. Say it."

"Told you so." He carefully placed the rest of the bagel in his mouth.

"How long does he plan to stay?" David asked.

"I don't know. I was going to discuss that with you."

"Oh?" David raised an eyebrow.

"Well, you see, since I just met him, I was hoping … he bought an open ticket, you see. So, whenever you get tired of him …"

"Terry," David said calmly. "He can stay as long as he wants. We've got the room. Steve will be moving back into his own house at the end of the week, and then Christian can sleep in the fourth bedroom. You won't need to bunk up. Who am I to stand in the way of a family reunion?"

"Thank you so much! You're a peach. Always have been."

"Not a problem, friend. You have a lot of time to make up for."

Terrence sighed happily. "I think I'm going to like being a dad." He laughed. "I never thought I would ever be saying that."

"Oh, how our pasts make fools of us all."

"Hey, guys," Christian said as he trudged into the room, rubbing his eyes. His hair was unruly and wild, and he wore a white t-shirt and striped blue boxers.

"Hey!" Terrence said, a wide, accepting smile on his face. "Can I get you something to eat?"

"That would be great," Christian replied, returning the smile. If Terrence was right, that smile would remain the whole day through. Christian had so far not been without it.

"Did you have a good night's rest?" David asked.

"You know, I really did. It's strange. I usually never sleep well at other people's houses, but …"

"Now see?" Terrence said. "Your body already knows this is your second home." He rose to get the box of pastries from atop the refrigerator.

"I think you're right," Christian agreed with that absolutely positive way of his.

Patrick watched from his window as his mother and Nanna pulled out of the drive and headed for Nanna's appointment with the doctor. It was yet another in a long line of doctor visits to try and control the old woman's nauseous stink.

Before they left, he watched humorously as Melinda chased Gayhound and another dog from the lawn. Horror of horrors! She finally understood Gayhound must truly be a *gay hound*, for it was another male dog he was humping. And right in the geraniums, too!

Once he was sure they were safely out of sight, he raced down the stairs, and then quickly out the sliding glass door to the backyard. He didn't think there was anyone in the neighborhood sympathetic to his mother's point of view, which consisted of hiding him from all civilization. Just to be safe, though, Patrick was watchful and on guard all the way to Cassie Bloom's house. His mother had been naive to think he wouldn't sneak out while she was out. Nanna had even warned her right there in front of him. But thankfully Melinda's simplicity won out.

"You won't do anything, will you?" she asked, still thinking he could not possibly lie to her. But then, maybe she knew. Maybe she secretly wanted him to sneak out. Of late, there had been an expression on her face, something new. Anticipation? Restlessness?

He also saw the way Melinda now looked at Nanna. Was it possible she was finally tiring of the old bitch? Even her voice while talking to Nanna was a bit reproachful, callous.

Did he imagine it, or was there a wink when she had said, "We'll be back in a couple hours, Patrick. Stay out of trouble, will you?"

Patrick stood at the door by the pool near the back of Cassie's house. The area looked a mess, as if there hadn't been anyone there for days to clean it. Leaves and twigs blemished the face of the pool water.

He waved and pounded on the glass as Cassie walked by. She stared at him, her eyes transforming from grief to elation.

"Patrick?" she said, as she came quickly to the door and slid it open. "What are you doing here? Your mother will have a fit!"

"She's not going to know. She took Nanna to the doctor. I have a couple of hours."

Cassie stared at him momentarily, playing with her diamond heart necklace, a wistful smile on her face. Her eyes, which seemed to be looking at something in another place, came back into focus. "Well, come in," she said. "Do you want something to drink?"

"No, I'm fine," he assured her as she led him into the TV room. "I just wanted to come over. I wanted to see you so I could apologize."

"Apologize?" Cassie questioned, as they sat on the sofa. "For what?"

"For all the trouble I've caused. For my mother being such a bitch. For my grandmother being such a Nazi."

"Patrick, darling," she said, taking his hand. "What trouble have you caused me?"

"I brought you into my fucked-up family's problems. I should never have even come to that party."

"Oh, rubbish! That party was fun, and you know it!"

He smiled. "Yeah, it was," he concurred. "I just wish it all had turned out different. I wish I was allowed to have a life." He rose and paced around the floor. "Sometimes I just hate my mother so much. I hate her! Why can't she see I want a life?"

"She thinks she's doing what's best for you. I can understand that desire. Every mother wants to shield her children from harm, and will break every rule to do it."

"But you wouldn't be like her."

"No," Cassie said, her gaze fading to somber reflection. Her voice became shallow and whispering. "But for my son, for Jason, I also did what I thought was right, and in the end it cost me the very person I was trying to protect."

Patrick sat again. "What happened?" he asked. He remembered Jason, but only vaguely. Melinda never let him play with the other boys on the street, not even Jason Bloom.

"My husband," she exhaled heavily. "My husband happened."

"His death?"

Cassie nodded, her eyes glassing over. "Jason was a compassionate, artistic, beautiful soul. My husband never saw that, though. He was always very tough on him, but Jason never held that against him. In fact, Jason looked on his father as if he were a god. But he wasn't. Not by a long shot."

"Jason was gay, wasn't he?"

"Yes," Cassie replied, with a smile. "Such a lovely boy, and I knew he was gay. I think I knew even before he was born. I could feel him moving around inside of me whenever disco came on the radio." She laughed, sad and worn. "When Jason finally came out with it one night, his father acted accepting. After all, Vera lived in the house, and he was fine with her. But Jackson was a great liar. He told me that night he was going to send Jason to a conversion camp ... or is it aversion?" She stopped and looked at Patrick. "Have you any idea the horrors children go through in those camps? It's psychiatric torture. And torture is something Jackson was very well-versed in, my boy."

Patrick now took hold of her hand as she began to cry.

"I begged with him to rethink things. We had a terrible fight. Punches were thrown. That's how bad it was. Vera was downstairs. She heard everything, and raced into our room just as Jackson threw me to the ground. I was bleeding. I had a gash on my cheek and a black eye. I was a mess."

"What did Vera do?"

"What any good friend would. She had heard us fight before, but this was different and she knew why. Jackson had barely turned around before she was on top of him, beating him with a poker from the fireplace. She nearly split his head in two."

"Oh my God!" Patrick exclaimed.

Cassie laughed through tears. "That's what we said."

"What did you do with the body?"

"He's still here," Cassie said, startling Patrick a bit. "Scattered about. That was a feat, let me tell you. Vera and I needed some solid thinkers. We were in no state to make decisions. So we called Becky and David, and they came up with a plan to hide him. In truth, I don't know where any of Jackson is. They took care of all that. Under a tree, under a bush … Vera and I have no idea."

"And they've covered it up all this time?"

"They're family. They're my true family. Jackson never understood the meaning of that word. When it's family, you take them for what they are. Love is the only thing."

"So Jason found out?"

"No. Jason never really knew, but he guessed that maybe I'd done something. He still looked at his father as some great individual, someone he needed to prove himself to. He never knew that Jackson was ready to pay a huge sum to try and have his own son changed from the person he was growing into. Of course, it would never work. Those camps, their methods, it's all hate. But still, Jason hasn't talked to me since."

"I'm so sorry, Cassie," Patrick said.

"Well," she replied, trying to regain her composure, "as Eleanor of Aquitaine says in *The Lion in Winter*, 'What family doesn't have its ups and downs?'"

Though Sandy wanted to go faster, she kept with the steady pace set by group leader Becky as the speed-walking group made their final trip around the neighborhood.

She had enjoyed it, more than she thought she would. They were a gossipy group, but Sandy knew if it had happened to someone else on the street, she would have been gossiping as well. They were not vindictive about it. They were just curious. All gossip is about curiosity. It's just about curiosity to varying degrees.

"You're married to a porn star!" Cock-Ring Girl quivered with excitement. "I tell all the girls at the bank I know a porn star! They're so jealous. I can tell!"

Of course, they spoke of other things as well as they made their great strides toward healthier living. Ruth spoke of her dead husband's desire to have his remains fed to zoo animals ("The man was crazy. That's all there is to it!"), Becky spoke of the hot new UPS guy (the other one had transferred, for obvious reasons), and one of the other ladies spoke to Ruth about Gayhound ("He's been very friendly with my German shepherd, Cuddles. Do you think they're an item?"). But it was Sandy who was the star. Her story could not be out-done. Most of the attention was paid to her. The whole group would hush and draw closer to hear anything she had to offer when she so much as said Steve's name in passing.

Cliff was out stretching on the driveway as the group approached David's house. His substantive thighs were barely contained by the tight running shorts he wore as he did lunges.

"That's some choice meat!" Ruth hollered before following her catcall with a whistle.

"Well, hey there, ladies!" Cliff called. He finished stretching as the ladies paused to say hello. "I might just join your speed-walking group, Becky," he said. "I can't keep up with David when he runs."

"You're welcome to," Becky said. "It's a good workout for me."

"Hey, Sandy," he greeted more somberly.

She nodded. "Hello, Cliff." It was an awkward acknowledgment.

Sensing the strained situation, Becky spoke up. "All right, come on, ladies. Let's finish this workout."

"I'll catch up," Sandy said, remaining with Cliff.

"Bring that hunk with you," Ruth called as they sped off.

"Oh, I'm coming for you, honey!" Cliff flirted. "Don't you worry!"

Ruth giggled, and the group's voices were soon inaudible.

Sandy and Cliff walked slowly in nervous silence.

"Are we talking again?" Cliff finally asked.

Sandy smiled. "I don't see why not. I don't think I was ever really mad at you or David. Like I told Steve, I understand the love behind this rather misguided action."

"Are you two going to work it out, then?"

"Of course we are," she said. "It's going to take time, but ... I miss him terribly, and he's only been out of the house for a week. I can't imagine a life without him."

"That's a relief," Cliff sighed. "I should never have mentioned the idea to Davey. He was only thinking of the two of you."

"I know." She wrapped her thin arm around his massive biceps. "And, to tell you the truth, I rather like the notoriety of having a husband so ... dangerous." She bit a fingernail, and looked at him as if she were an embarrassed little girl telling a secret she knew would get her in trouble.

He laughed. "You know what? So does David."

"What can I say? We're publicity whores."

"Nothing wrong with that. Doesn't mean you're not also good people. Everyone needs to be noticed, right?"

"We've got quite a group of characters on this street, huh?" she said, looking about.

"We could be a book. Maybe David could write it."

"It'd be bestseller."

James stripped naked, and then slid into his army running shorts. There was a ferocity in him right now. He had a mission, and there was nothing that was going to stand in his way. He was charging for the truth like a battering ram.

He grabbed the guitar by the bed and raced down the stairs and out the door in his bare feet. His face was strong and set with steely determination. It had been building in his guts all night and had eventually pushed its way upward.

He had never felt more courageous.

There were a few people out, doing yard work or walking their dogs. Each one of them stopped and watched him literally pound the pavement with his strong feet. The guitar-wielding army man had a small audience behind him as he made his way to David's house. He would not be turned away or ignored.

He marched into the front yard and snatched one of the lounge chairs Terrence had used to watch him jog by every day. Putting one leg up on the chair, he rested the guitar on his hip, as he stood and stared at the house. The small crowd watched from the street; some wandered onto the lawn as well. Mumbles and whispers surfed over their heads.

James cleared his voice and began singing along to the chords he strummed.

David heard an off-key but sweet voice singing from somewhere nearby as he typed out his latest piece for *Gay Men's Fitness*. "Abs and Ass: The Seven Deadly Sins."

"What the hell?" he said to himself. Though it sounded like the brooding, introspective music that Rick liked, surely he would not play it so loud. It wasn't coming from inside the house anyway.

He rose and went to the window. James was out on the lawn, nearly naked, holding a guitar. He had brought a fan club with him.

"Ricky!" David yelled, as he descended the stairs in his boxers.

"I hear it," Rick said, coming into the living room. "What's he doing?"

"He's serenading you, dumbass. Does that song mean anything?"

Rick almost smiled. "It's a song by Iron & Wine. 'Each Coming Night.' I was trying to get him hooked on them."

"Sounds like you succeeded," David posited as the two watched out the window at the concert.

"Yeah. Well, it's not going to be this easy for him."

Rick went out onto the lawn, too angry to even worry about the crowd. Normally the sight of so many people with their attention focused on him would have made his hand automatically rise to cover his eye patch, but he was not concerned with that at the moment.

As he sped at James over the grass in his shorts and polo, the guitarist put down his instrument. It fell with a soft thud to the ground.

"Rick," James whispered, his face a mixture of hope and fear.

His acknowledgment was met only by Rick's fist. James fell backward onto the grass. The crowd gasped in excitement.

James wiped at the blood from his busted lip. "Rick," he said. "I'm sorry."

"Not yet," Rick warned. "I'll forgive you in a few minutes, but not yet."

"What? Why not?"

But Rick jumped on him, punching and cursing.

"Son of a bitch! Goddamn piece of shit! Motherfucker!"

They rolled over and over in the grass, Rick hitting, shouting, and cussing, James shielding and grunting.

David stood at his door, staring in disbelief. "Our Ricky, taking on the army," he said to himself.

Finally, they stopped. Rick fell off James and onto the grass beside him. They both stared into the sky, breathing heavily. The crowd was quiet and waiting.

"Are you through?" James asked. "Is it all out?"

"I think so," Rick answered. Shortly, though, he hit James again in the arm. "Sorry," he said. "Now it's all out."

"I'm forgiven?"

"You're on your way."

James rose on his elbow and faced Rick. "I'll never do it to you again. I am a gay man. I'm completely out now. Ballser is sure to tell everyone, and I'm okay with that."

"Are you going to hate me? Did I force you out before you were ready?"

"No," James said, taking a blade of grass and tickling Rick's lips. "This feels right. This was my time to come out … And I could never hate you."

They kissed gently. The crowd around them sighed with expressions of satisfied play-goers.

James reached for the eye patch, but Rick caught his hand.

"I want to see you, Rick," he said. "All of you."

Rick's hand dropped, and James pulled off the patch, revealing the darkened flesh. Rick closed his other eye in anticipation of rejection. Instead, he felt the touch of lips on his most hated physical attribute.

"You are beautiful," James whispered. "Open your eye and look at me."

Rick did as he was asked.

"You are beautiful."

Rick buried his head in James chest, and the two of them lay there until the crowd dispersed. Then they rose and strolled to the sidewalk, where they sat facing the street, an easy comfort settling over them.

Melinda was trying very hard not to hear her mother rant as they drove down Jasper Lane toward home. It wasn't easy. Her nerves were completely on edge. The old woman's voice was a tiny dagger that kept stabbing at her head with slow, twisting turns.

"Leaving him here was a mistake," Nanna griped. "Sometimes I believe you don't know a thing about mothering … and you didn't get that from me."

"Well, Mother, what am I supposed to do?" Melinda replied. "You need me to take you to the doctor. I can't lock him in his room."

"We need to get some of the church members to come over and watch him. And as for me, I'm looking at a nice golf cart to drive around in. You won't have to worry about me no more, girlie."

"Mother, you can't drive around the city in a golf cart."

"Oh, yes, I can!" she squawked. "You just mind your own business. I'll worry about my means of transportation. You need to get that boy in line. We need some type of Christian intervention. There are camps, you know."

Melinda closed her off, instead focusing on the crowd that surrounded David's yard. She tried to see through the people, but was unable to do so. Suddenly, she wished to be among them, whatever they were doing.

She parked in the drive and left her mother to continue yacking alone as she quickly fled into the house.

"Melinda! Melinda!" Nanna yelled, having a good deal of trouble getting out of the SUV.

Melinda ascended the stairs and knocked on Patrick's door.

"Patrick, are you there?"

"Yes, Mom," he replied curtly from inside. "I didn't escape."

She sighed with sadness. He would have raced to her once, back when they would read Bible stories at night. He had smiled so often then. What had happened? What had she done? Was Cassie right? Had she smothered him the same way her own mother had?

She shook her head. One shouldn't think such thoughts about their own parents.

"Melinda!" Nanna screeched downstairs.

Melinda pretended to listen to the continuous jabbering as she walked past her mother and put on some coffee. Occasionally she would give a "Yes, Mother," or "Of course, Mother," but she wished she could be anywhere else.

With her coffee in hand, she opted to drink it on the porch rather than in the kitchen with her mother.

"What's gotten into you?" Nanna barked.

Melinda stood on the porch near the wood railing, drinking her expensive coffee. It really wasn't that good. Why had she paid so much for it?

As she continued to drown her mother from her mind, the irritating sound of her phlegmy voice scratching the atmosphere, Melinda's eyes again were drawn in the direction of the Boys' home where the crowd had been assembled. They were all gone now, but there, sitting on the sidewalk talking, were the army man, James, and the one with the eye patch.

James was once again shirtless. Melinda felt a surge of uncontrollable anger. *Shirtless!* After all her stern looks of disapproval!

She threw the coffee mug to the porch. As it hit, it shattered into pieces. Nanna stopped talking immediately, and stared at her from the door in shock.

Melinda sped across her perfect lawn, across the street under the trees, heading for the two men with an anger that had been growing for some time- much longer than even she knew.

"You!" she shouted at James, pointing her finger as if she were throwing darts.

James and Rick looked at her, startled, as she rapidly approached them. They looked behind them, unsure of whom she was addressing.

"You!" she yelled again. Her teeth were gritted. She gritted her teeth, trembling.

"Yes?" James said, as he and Rick slowly rose to their feet.

"What are you doing? Have you no decency?" She stood in front of them, heaving. Her face was red with rage.

"What is she talking about?" Rick asked James.

James rolled his eyes. "I don't know. What is it, Mrs. Gold?"

"You know what it is!"

"I really don't," he answered calmly.

"You move into the neighborhood, you flaunt your lifestyles-both of you ..."

"No one is flaunting anything," James protested.

"Then you run around almost naked after I have asked you many, many times not to go about so ... exposed ..."

"Mrs. Gold, I beg your pardon, but you've never said two words to me. You just stand at the end of your drive and watch me."

Her mouth dropped in incomprehension at the accusation. "I do *not* watch you! Why would I?" she screamed, as she began to shake uncontrollably. "I have a wonderful husband! He's a marvelous man! How dare you imply ..."

"Melinda, maybe you should calm down," Rick recommended, sensing that she might have an aneurism if she continued.

"I will not calm down!" she shouted, as she started hitting both of them with balled hands. It was harmless, and James succeeded in grabbing her wrists.

Other neighbors were now coming out of their homes and gardens to watch. Two shows in one day! This was special.

"You let go of her, you sodomite!" Nanna bellowed from the porch. Patrick came out onto the porch to see what the ruckus was about.

"Shut up, Mother! I'll handle this!" Melinda screamed back. "This is my life," she said, returning her attention to the two men. "My life!" She was on the verge of righteous tears.

"Who said it wasn't?" James asked, letting go of her wrists.

She looked at him as if no one had ever agreed with her before. "Everyone says so!" she continued after a pause. "They all do! They imply it. I try to be a good mother, to be the wife, mother, and daughter they all deserve-but what about me? When do I get what I deserve?"

She collapsed onto the concrete and buried her head in her hands. James and Rick sat down cautiously on each side of her.

"You know," she whimpered. "I was never allowed to look at guys who looked like you. I was always taught I should suppress what I wanted, that my desire was sinful. To look at someone and want ... was sinful. So, I married the first gosh-darned jerk that came along!"

"Frank?" Rick asked.

"Uh-huh," she squeaked, sniffling. "And now I have this family. This family that drives me crazy! A family I never really wanted in the first place."

"But you love them, right?" Rick tried comforting her, putting his hand on her back.

"I have to, don't I?" She looked at him with reticence before standing again. "Can I tell you something?" she asked, turning to face them.

"Sure," James shrugged.

"I don't think I know what love is. It sounds like a bad line, but it's true. I look at my life and all I see is discontent ... everywhere! I have a son who resents me, a husband whom I *know* is not spending all those late nights at work, and a mother I hate!" She put her hand to her mouth in shock.

James and Rick glanced at one another. Their eyes conferred to one another that, yes, Melinda Gold just might be crazy.

"Did I just say that?" she whispered.

Rick nodded.

"Is my mother still on the porch?"

James nodded.

"Fuck!" she screamed, scaring birds from trees and causing dogs to bark.

"Melinda!" Nanna belched forth.

Patrick smiled, however. It was possibly the toothiest grin that had ever crossed his face.

"You have your god, right?" Rick suggested. "He loves you still. There's some love, right?"

"Oh," she moaned in disgust. "Fuck him too!"

James and Rick sat in silence as the resident Bible-thumper of Jasper Lane walked with angry footfalls back to her home.

"Shame on you, Melinda!" Nanna chided.

Patrick simply stared at her with interest.

"Shut up, Mother!" she said to the old woman once again, and slammed the screen door behind her.

Steve walked into his house to the sound of laughter coming from the kitchen. Thankfully, he would be moving back very soon.

He had found a new job, a real job in sales. He would, in truth, miss the studio. Or rather, he would miss the money that it brought in. He had also made some strong acquaintances there. Good people like Evan and Gabriel, who were honest and friendly. Sandy would have liked them.

But sales was fine. It would at least get things back on track with Sandy, even if they did have to move from Jasper Lane.

In the kitchen, he found Sandy sitting at the island with Cliff, both of them laughing and relaxed, with Heinekens in their hands.

"Hey, Steve," Cliff greeted, taking a drink.

Steve nodded to him with a confused smile. "Hey, honey," he said to his wife.

"What do you say we go out to eat tonight?" she asked. "Chinese?"

"Uh, sure," he answered. The dinner invitation made his heart leap.

"Well," Cliff said, rising from his stool. "I better go. Dave will be wondering where I went. Thanks for the Heinekens, Sandy."

"See you, Cliff," Sandy yelled after him. As he made his way out of the kitchen, he gave Steve a friendly tap on the shoulder.

Sandy went to the fridge and grabbed a beer for her husband.

"Thanks," he said, as he twisted off the cap, still in a state of bewilderment. "I've got great news! I got a new job," he told her.

"Oh," she said. She seemed disappointed.

"It's in sales," he continued. "Isn't that what you wanted?"

"It's ... it's fine," she replied.

"I thought you'd be ecstatic."

"I am ... it's fine ..." There was a long pause as she studied him. "Actually, no, it's not."

"What?"

"It's not fine," she reiterated. "Listen, Steve, there was a message on the voice mail after I returned from walking today."

He broke into a cold sweat. What kind of bad news was this?

"It was a woman from the Gay Porn Wives Club, and ..."

"The what?" He stared at her, eyes wide.

"The Gay Porn Wives Club. It's this group of women who are married to men who act in gay-for-pay movies ... like you," she explained cheerfully.

He sat down on a stool at the island and absentmindedly took a drink from the bottle.

"They've invited us to a banquet next weekend, you see. They're giving you an award. They love you!" She was giddy. A wide grin swept across her face.

"Are you serious?"

"Cliff is getting an award, too. They don't only give awards to other gay-for-pay actors, but that's how the group started."

"Seriously?"

"Yes, Steve, I'm serious!" she exclaimed. "So ... I can't believe I'm going to say this ... I don't think you should take the sales position."

He kept staring at her dumbfounded.

"It's up to you," she said. "But you're right, the money is great, and it might not be so bad for us if you do a few more films until the baby is born."

She was fidgeting as if she thought he might yell and curse at her.

"But you wanted me to quit," he said. "You kicked me out over it."

"I know, and I'm sorry about that. I'll make it up to you."

"It's that easy? 'Oh, well, all's forgiven?' You don't consider it cheating?"

"Well, I'm still sorting that one out. But you don't love these guys. And let's face it, what they're zeroing in on is an area of no interest to me."

"I see," he responded. "So you want me to continue ..."

"Acting ..."

"Getting butt-fucked ..."

Sandy watched him intently. Just like everyone else, Steve had his moods. Thinking back, though, she had never really seen him angry. Could this open the flood gates?

He took a long drink from his bottle, and slammed it down on the island. He sat quietly for a moment. He appeared to be having a silent argument in his mind.

"Okay," he said. "Let's go get some Chinese."

CHAPTER 13

Melinda had been on edge all week. Since her outburst on the street a few days before, she felt as if it would be impossible for her to continue on in the manner in which she had lived. Not because of embarrassment or how she might be viewed, but because she had let loose something within herself. Her flare-up at Rick and James was merely a tremor compared to the earthquake that was inside her. She was frightened of it, of what she had said, but, at the same time ... *it felt so good.*

Nanna, though spiteful and vicious, had the ability to read her daughter very well. What she saw disturbed her. Melinda seemed to be undergoing an undesirable shift. Nanna watched her for any more unusual signs. Strangely, though, not a word was said. Nanna's suspicions were transmitted through her dour expression.

Patrick was right, Melinda concluded. Nanna *did* look like a turtle! Why hadn't she ever noticed that before? And turtles were such ugly creatures-why couldn't her mother have looked like a swan or something more graceful?

The way she shuffled around was driving Melinda insane. She was quite capable of picking up her feet, and yet she *shuffled!* It was nearly as irritating as fingers on a chalkboard.

As Melinda drank her coffee at the kitchen table, Nanna shuffled, stared, and farted past. Melinda closed her eyes in an effort to shield the cold rage she felt.

Why couldn't Nanna have stayed upstairs all morning?

"He's been out there all morning," the old woman said, nodding in the direction of the pool. "He's up to something."

Melinda shot her an irritated glance. "He's not up to anything, Mother. Just leave him alone!"

"What's wrong with you? What did those two sodomites say to you?"

Those two 'sodomites', as she had called them, had shown her more kindness and understanding in a few minutes than Nanna had her whole life.

"Didn't you say you were going somewhere this morning, Mother?" Melinda asked impatiently.

"I called a cab. Should be here any minute."

"Well, then I should think you would want to be waiting for it ... out there," she motioned with her head, "... on the porch."

Nanna gave her another curious glare, and then shuffled off.

Melinda returned her absent stare back to the wall. The crucifix clock caught her eye. It was such a bossy, annoying thing. She couldn't remember why she made the decision to buy it.

Melinda put her mug down, and walked to the wall, her hands on her hips. She spent the next few minutes grappling between an emerging truth and a fading ideal. In the end, the truth won.

She grabbed the clock and indifferently dropped it in the trash can.

"Honey," David called, "it's almost time to go. We need to leave soon if we want to get there in time. The limo is waiting."

He straightened his black, silk tie in the mirror in Steve and Sandy's living room. He hated suits. In fact, he hated clothes altogether. He was quite content to type out his living in his boxer briefs. It was approaching noon, and the banquet would start at four at a small university a couple of hours away.

"I'm so excited about this!" Sandy giggled, as she helped Steve with his tie.

"Who'd have thunk it, huh?" Steve said. "Me, getting an award for getting my ass fucked."

"It's the acting," Sandy corrected. "It's an award for the acting. You gave a good performance. Utterly convincing."

"Wasn't much acting to it. It hurt like hell."

"You straight guys are such wimps," David teased. "Besides, the ladies love you."

"And you've got that fan site now too," Sandy gleamed proudly.

"Two of them," David corrected.

"There's two now?" Her eyes widened in delight.

"Look at you," Steve laughed. "You're eating this up. You are so my porn manager."

"It's fun," she defended herself. "You're a star!"

"Starfucker," Steve kidded.

"What is he doing? Cliff!" David yelled.

"Coming!" Cliff hollered back.

Cliff walked into the room half-dressed. His tuxedo was a mess-the cummerbund was undone, and the tie was still hanging loosely around his neck.

"You're supposed to be dressed!" David chided.

"Well, I would be but ..." He held out his arms to the side to reveal the tuxedo was a few sizes too small.

"You didn't see this when you tried it on?"

Cliff looked at him guiltily.

"You didn't try it on, did you?"

"You know I hate doing that! I just wanted to get it and get out of there."

"So you spent all that money on something that will never fit?"

Cliff smiled innocently. "It was a used tux shop. This was the largest they had."

"Cliff, honey, you're a gorilla. You're huge! There is no one in three states as big as you. I thought you got fitted."

"In a week? You were already set. You had that tux from the costume for the Fourth party. Steve, they can't fit someone and make a tux for them in less than a week."

"Okay, okay," David sighed. "So, what'll we do?"

"I've got an idea," Sandy said. "And the ladies of the Gay Porn Wives Club will love it!"

She walked to Cliff as if it were an inspection. "The pants are nice and tight. They show your package and ass off great. Don't wear the jacket."

"That's no problem. I couldn't fit into it."

She pulled the tie from around his neck and threw it and the cummerbund on the floor, then opened his shirt a bit more, and finally, ripped off the sleeves. His arms looked even larger the normal. The effect was very satisfactory.

"Huh," Steve and David said in unison.

"All right," Cliff grinned. "I'm ready to go now."

He held out his arm to David, and they walked to the door. Steve and Sandy followed.

Cassie sat on her porch in white cotton slacks and a pink blouse. The large, white wicker swing she sat in creaked as the last breaths of summer air wafted past her. She could look out over the entire length of the neighborhood from the swing, like some queen watching over her realm. Jackson had always liked the spot. The hill on which the house was situated gave it an aura of importance and grandeur, lending it the appearance of a small castle. Cassie was less impressed by it. It didn't make her feel privileged at all. Instead, she mostly felt lonely.

"What are you doing out here all alone?" Vera inquired, as she stepped out onto the porch with two glasses of Chardonnay. Cassie took one with an appreciative smile.

"Just thinking," she replied.

"I know that look, sweetie. What are you *thinking* about?" Vera positioned herself beside Cassie on the swing. Her hair was swept up in a silver turban, pinned together with a pearl brooch, and she wore a silver and purple silk kimono.

"Jason called," Cassie answered, taking a sip of her Chardonnay.

"Well, God bless!" Vera exclaimed in a hushed tone. "What did he say, honey?"

"He wants to talk about things." Her eyes were watering.

"Maybe you should tell him, Cassie. Maybe it's time."

"No, Vera. I'm not sending you to jail over something I should have done."

"Jason wouldn't send me to jail, darling. You think that boy would turn me in? No, especially not after he learns why it happened."

"He did love you," Cassie said with a smile, as she grasped her friend's hand. "You should tell him."

"Maybe one day," Cassie said, "but not any time soon. He's off to travel Europe for a year, and then, when he returns, he says he wants to get together."

"That boy!" Vera shook her head. "He's going to make you wait a year in limbo wondering what he's thinking? You'll be pulling your hair out by the end!"

"He always was a tease," Cassie said.

"Just like his mother." Vera slapped her gently on the shoulder. Cassie laughed.

"I missed having a young man in the house, Vera." She stared vacantly onto the street.

"Is that why you offered the job to Patrick?"

"I suppose it was. I just saw how unhappy he was, and it reminded me of how unhappy Jason was before he came out, before he was able to love himself."

"Jason's leaving was not your fault, honey. Neither was Patrick's."

"Maybe not," Cassie stated, though she seemed unconvinced. She shook herself from her melancholy. "Where do you think they put him?" she asked, suddenly awake again.

"Hmmm?"

"Jackson," Cassie clarified. "Do you think David and Becky buried some of him under the rose bush over there?"

"Possibly," Vera answered. "They are beautiful, and the man probably made great fertilizer."

"He *was* full of shit." They laughed. "What body part do you think it is? If it's under the rose bush, I mean?"

"Eeewww, Cassie!"

"Just take a guess. A stab in the dark."

"What do *you* think it is?"

"His liver. Definitely. Remember, he drank a lot more than I do. Gin blossoms ... yuck!"

"And how exactly do gin blossoms translate to a rose bush?"

"They both bloom."

As they guffawed at the disturbing image, Becky came speed-walking up the path to the house. "Yoo-hoo!" she hollered.

"Hi, Becky," Cassie greeted.

"Hello, ladies," Becky said, as cheerfully as ever. "Are you two up to anything?"

"No good," Vera answered.

"Well, fantastic! Then you'll fit right in. Terrence and the Boys are having a margarita party on their front lawn. What say we all hop on over?"

"Sounds good to me," Cassie responded, rising from the swing.

"I hear that," Vera chimed in. "But I'm bringing the Chardonnay. I hate tequila!"

The Boys lounged on the lawn, shirtless. They wore nothing but shades, trunks, and expressions of contentment. Terrence lay back in his usual chair, looking up at the blue sky. His hand held his margarita lazily. Christian lay nearby on a blanket he had spread on the grass, and James and Rick lay on their own separate blanket. Rick's head rested on James' stomach in complete comfort. Terrence had won the music coin toss, so Madonna blared from inside the house.

"This is fantastic!" Christian exclaimed. "I'm going to miss lying out here."

"You're here for another week, right?" Rick asked.

Neither of them moved a muscle. Conversations were allowed, but sunbathing was their top priority.

"Yeah. One more week," he responded.

"I wish you could stay longer," Terrence admitted. "I'm having fun playing dad."

Christian grinned. "I'm having a great time, too, but I think Mom is missing me."

"When do you think you'll be back?" Terrence asked. He lifted his head to take a drink.

"I was thinking Christmas. Is that okay?"

"That would be perfect!" Terrence exclaimed. It was clear he was hoping Christian might suggest that particular holiday. "You'll love this place at Christmas."

James began shaking his hips to "Music," disturbing Rick's comfort. Rick smacked him playfully on the belly.

"Oh, sigh," Terrence moaned. "Ricky, now that you're moving in with James, it's just going to be David and me again. I kind of liked having so many people in the house. It reminded me of college, living in the frat."

"You were never in a fraternity," Rick said.

"Well, not officially," Terrence agreed. "But I spent enough nights in them."

Christian laughed. "Awesome," he said. "That's my dad."

"Have you got all of your things packed up?" Terrence gestured towards Rick with his margarita.

"Yeah, that took about ten minutes this morning," Rick replied.

"We need to get you some more stuff," James added. "Three boxes of CDs and a few articles of clothing-that's just sad."

"Yoo-hoo!" Becky's voice shouted over the music, as she, Cassie, and Vera approached.

"Hey, ladies," James greeted, as the Boys all opened their eyes and sat up.

"We heard you were having a little afternoon get-together over here," Cassie said. "Mind if we join in?"

"That would be marvelous!" Terrence said. "Let me fix you some drinks." He rose from the chair and went inside to get more supplies.

James jumped up to get the other lawn chairs.

Cassie and Vera wasted no time having fun, as they began to dance to the music until the chairs and drinks were brought to them.

"What a lovely summer day," Cassie said, sitting back in her chair.

"Glorious," Vera agreed. "Especially with such handsome young men here to help us relax." She winked at Christian, who grinned in embarrassment.

"What is this?" Cassie exclaimed. A very slow-moving vehicle was creeping down the street.

"It looks like a golf cart," Terrence said, lifting the shades from his eyes.

"Is that Melinda's mother?" Becky asked. "Did she buy a golf cart?"

"Why would that old hag buy a golf cart?" Cassie asked.

"Do old women golf?" Terrence wrinkled his nose.

"Mark my words, ladies and gentlemen," Cassie said, rising to her feet with drink in hand. "Something's about to happen. We're going to get a show. I can feel it."

"Oh, honey! That's a wicked little smile on your face," Vera said with a smile of her own.

Melinda came out onto the porch, arms folded, as Nanna parked the tan golf cart in the driveway. The old woman rose from her seat with a grunt and shuffled to the house.

"Mother, what is this?" Melinda asked, her brow furrowed in confusion.

"I told you I needed a ride of my own. This way I won't need to depend on you for a ride everywhere, and you can keep an eye on your brat." She stood on the sidewalk, looking back proudly at her new purchase as if it were a gold Cadillac.

"But where did you find the money?"

Coincidentally or not, Patrick chose that particular moment to come racing out the door in a gasping panic.

"Patrick, what's wrong?" Melinda asked, holding him by the shoulders.

He pulled away from her. "My money!" he exclaimed. "My money! It's gone! All of it!"

"What money?"

"The money I had saved from working for Cassie," he said breathlessly. In his eyes was a desperation Melinda couldn't remember ever seeing. It broke her heart. But then her mind grasped in full the wrong that had been done him.

Melinda shot a quick, accusatory glare at her mother. "Mother, you didn't!"

"That money wasn't his," Nanna defended herself, as she edged closer to her new golf cart. A selfish awareness overtook her expression. "He lied to get it. He doesn't deserve it. God knows I need this fine machine more than anything he could buy with it."

"Mother! How could you!"

"Don't you judge me, young lady! Don't you dare judge me! I deserve a little something for all the troubles I've had to deal with. With all the years I had to deal with you and your sister—and with him as well. Why, if I hadn't been around, that boy would have done walked all over you. I more or less raised him, and you know it! Huh. You're barely a mother at all! You haven't got what it takes!"

Melinda was mortified by her mother's diatribe. She had no idea how to correctly—and appropriately—deal with the fury. Behind her, Patrick was seething. His fists were clenched in rage, and he glared at the old woman with such menace that she climbed into the cart and started it. She moved faster than anyone expected.

"You bitch!" he yelled.

As he leaped off the porch, Melinda grabbed him.

"No, Patrick! Not here!"

The neighborhood was watching. The Boys across the way stood and gawked with Cassie, Vera, and Becky. Did it even matter anymore what they thought?

"I'm going to kill her!" he shouted. And Melinda not only believed him, she empathized with him.

"Patrick, no! We'll find another way!"

Nanna pulled out of the drive, heading down the street at a turtle's pace.

"Let me go!" Patrick yelled, as he tore himself out of his mother's grasp and took off after Nanna.

Melinda fell back into her manicured bushes. She was on her feet again in an instant, chasing after her son, calling his name in a dog-whistle's pitch.

Nanna looked over her shoulder, determined to escape with her prize. "Stay away from me, boy!" she bellowed.

She tried to weave, thinking that she might be able to lose him. She crouched down behind the wheel like a granny boxcar racer.

"Mother! Patrick!" Melinda cried running after both of them.

Cassie and the lawn party followed the parade of absurdity down the street. Gayhound, too, began nipping at the wheels of the cart.

"Shoo! Git, you queer dog!" Nanna spit.

There was no real need to run, though. Patrick caught up with Nanna within seconds. She fought him, slapping and biting his hands away. As Melinda arrived, Patrick tossed Nanna into Melinda's arms and took control of the moving cart. Melinda held tight to her mother.

"What are you doing with my cart?" Nanna raged. Gayhound barked at her in ferocious yelps.

Patrick put it in reverse, and proceeded back to the house at a more intense speed.

"You bought it with my money!" Patrick clarified. "It's mine to do with what I want!"

Nanna fought with Melinda to free herself, and at last succeeded by kicking her daughter in the shin. Melinda went down, holding her leg as the old woman took off after Patrick.

"Go, Patrick!" cheered Cassie and the lawn party, as they galloped alongside the cart with their drinks.

He pulled into the drive once again, and then plowed through Melinda's flowers and perfect yard.

"No!" Melinda shrieked, still far behind, holding her injured shin while Gayhound tugged on her pant-suit.

Patrick disappeared from view behind the house, mowing down the fence to the pool area.

"No! No!" Nanna screamed, realizing his intent.

Nanna screamed in rage as the crowd heard a large splash from the back-yard, using more curse words than Melinda had ever heard in her life.

Patrick walked back around to the front of the house with a look of extreme satisfaction. He passed his shocked mother on the lawn as his grandmother's foul rant continued in the back.

He walked across the street, proudly, his smile expanding with each step. Cassie was laughing so hard that she was crying. The rest of the crowd exploded into cheers and applause.

"Lordy, Patrick!" Vera guffawed. "You just let it all out, didn't you?"

"Cassie," he said. "I'd like my job back if it's still open. My mother's not going to stop me. I'm making my own choices now."

"Good for you, Patrick," Cassie said, hugging him so hard he lost his breath. "You bet you can have your job back!"

"We missed you, baby!" Vera added.

"I missed you, too," he said, squeezing Vera's hand.

"Uh, Patrick," Rick said, as he gestured with a nod at Nanna as she approached him from behind. Melinda was a few feet behind her.

As Patrick turned around, the old lady smacked him so hard across the face that his nose immediately began to bleed.

"You little shit!" she hissed.

For Melinda, that was it. She grabbed her mother by the shoulder, whirled her around, and laid a loud slap on her.

"Don't you ever touch my son again!" she screamed vehemently.

Patrick had been stunned by Nanna's smack, but he was even more shocked by his mother's response to it.

Nanna looked at her daughter, eyes wide and frightened.

"You go get your stuff packed together," Melinda ordered. "You're leaving tonight." She turned to Cassie. "Do you think you might be able to spare Patrick for a few hours so he can get a golf cart out of my pool?"

"Sure," Cassie nodded. "Congratulations, Melinda! Looks like you just found yourself."

Melinda looked at the group. "Thank you," she said to all of them.

Melinda pushed her mother across the street and into the house. Gayhound was dragged along as well, refusing to give up his hold on Melinda's pant leg.

The entire neighborhood stood staring in astonishment.

"I so just got a flash of Darth Vader throwing the Emperor down the shaft in *Jedi*," Terrence posited.

"Totally," Christian agreed, his smile as wide as ever.

"Well, lovers," Cassie said. "It seems as if Melinda might be ready to let us accept her into our little family." She threw her arm around Patrick as they walked with the others back to the Boys' lawn. The afternoon was just beginning.

Everything was just getting started.

Epilogue

Cliff and David's wedding was an intimate affair on the Fourth of July the next summer. Sandy had come up with the festive idea.

"It would be a perfect Independence Day party!" she exclaimed, her eyes wide with hope.

It was decided that, instead of the usual costumed extravaganza the Jones usually held, there would be a covenant, a joining, between two men who had come to love one another dearly.

The backyard was furnished with chairs and tables, a large gazebo was assembled near the house, and flowers were draped everywhere. It looked and smelled like a fairytale.

The reception would be held there as well, although it would most likely spill out into the street. The whole neighborhood would be invited to that, as well as many others the couple knew from their active social life. But the wedding itself was for family only-whether blood or kindred.

Steve and Sandy were the extent of the wedding party. The two grooms walked down the aisle together to "At This Point in My Life" by Tracy Chapman as their mothers waited for them at the gazebo. Cliff nearly had to double over so that his tiny mother could give him a peck on the cheek. He had even suffered through a tuxedo fitting for the special event.

After the ceremony, the party began in earnest. Steve once again had control of the sound system, piping a cacophony of music throughout the neighborhood. David and Cliff cut the cake and danced to Etta James.

"Oh, Puh-leeease!" Terrence was overheard to say.

After the toasts and dedications were finished, everyone happily milled and mingled. There was an open bar, after all, and a crowd soon began to grow. Soon it became a rowdy neighborhood-wide festival. Jasper Lane was a sea of joyous celebration, which would continue well into the early hours of the morning.

Melinda approached the happy couple, a small glass of punch in her hand. She wore a conservative pink gown and a string of pearls.

"I want to thank you for inviting me," she said, her smile still nervous and uncertain. She knew they all accepted her, but it was an adjustment for her all the same.

"We're glad you could come, Melinda," David said. "Are you having fun?"

"Yes," she said. "It's lovely."

"I saw Patrick over there. Is that his girlfriend?"

"Yes," she replied. "They met at freshman orientation last month. She's going to Hanover College as well. They seem to have hit it off."

"You must be so proud of him," Cliff said. "Hanover's a good school."

"It is, and I am. He's helped me out so much since the divorce." She covered her mouth. "I'm sorry. I shouldn't be talking about my bad luck on such a … happy occasion."

"You're fine," David said, touching her gently on the arm. "We're all friends now."

She liked this, and nodded. "Where are you honeymooning?" she asked.

David and Cliff looked at one another. "A gay resort," David answered, "in Bermuda."

"Oh," Melinda said. "There are gay resorts?"

"Patrick!" Cassie shouted in greeting, as she and Vera extravagantly made their way across the steady stream of guests. They each held two drinks and were dressed in excessive finery. Their hats were large and boisterous, their gowns billowy and light.

"Hey!" Patrick said with a wide grin. They embraced lovingly.

"Where have you been, young man?" Cassie inquired. "I've hardly seen you all summer. My pool is a mess!"

"The boys from the night club don't do it justice, baby!" Vera interjected.

"Sorry. I've been getting everything ready for school next year," he answered.

"And your mother is paying for all of it. Will wonders never cease!" Cassie said. "I think it's wonderful!"

"She's finally letting me live my life. Things have gotten so much better since Nanna and Dad left. And you know what? I don't feel at all bad for wishing them gone."

"Good. I'm glad, honey. You deserve your happiness. You've earned it."

"This is Rachel," Patrick said, introducing his first-ever girlfriend.

"She's beautiful!" Cassie gleamed.

Rachel bowed her head shyly. "Patrick's told me all about you," she said sweetly.

"You vengeful boy!" Cassie joked. "Lies! All lies, I say!"

"Anyway," Patrick said, laughing. "I'll catch up with you later. Mom is standing over there all alone. I'm going to go comfort her for a few minutes. Everyone still kind of freaks her out."

"You're a good son," Vera said.

"Don't worry, Patrick," Cassie assured him. "When you're off at college we'll get her thawed out. She's going to feel comfortable living here again. I promise. She's part of the family, my dear."

Patrick kissed her and Vera on their cheeks before leaving hand-in-hand with Rachel.

"How exciting for him," Cassie said as they watched him walk away.

"Jason comes home next month, hon," Vera offered, sensing what Cassie was thinking. "You'll have a young man in the house again."

"For a bit, anyway."

They walked through the crowd, arms linked, exchanging nods and pleasantries with the other guests.

"It will be interesting to see how things turn out between us. It's been so long. I'm scared as hell, Vera. I don't know what I'll do if he still hates me."

"Oh, honey," Vera comforted, putting an arm over Cassie's shoulder. After a moment's silence between them, she spoke again. "You'll never guess what I found the other day."

"What, sweetie? Tell me what you found."

"A bone ... right there under the rose bush. Just peaking up from the soil like a curious earth worm."

Cassie's eyes flew wide, and she stared at Vera. "Do you think it's Jackson?"

"I'm not sure, honey. It was sort of short and crooked." She paused. "Maybe it was his dick."

Cassie kept her gaze for as long as she could, until they both doubled over in laughter, bumping clumsily into those around them.

"I knew he was going to do it!" Steve grinned at Rick. Sandy stood beside her husband with Amy tucked lovingly in her arms. Their daughter was only a few months old.

"When did you ask?" Sandy asked James.

"Last night," he replied. "I've been wanting to do it for a while."

"Yeah, it was real romantic," Rick said sarcastically, with an affectionate grin. He had donned a flashy purple-sequined eye patch that James had bought him for the occasion. "We were watching reruns of *Little House* and he says-through chunks of popcorn-'Hey, why don't we get married?' How could I say no to that?"

"He didn't think I was serious at first," James said, hitting Rick lightly on the shoulder.

"Well, you set the bar pretty high after our first few dates and your other romantic gestures."

"I'll make it up to you."

"Naw," Rick said. "I liked it just fine. It was perfect." He kissed James softly, momentarily forgetting the other guests.

"Aw," Sandy sighed. "That's so sweet."

"Don't tell anyone just yet, though," James said. "This is David and Cliff's day. We don't want to take that from them."

"Our lips are sealed," Steve assured them. "Congratulations!"

"To you too," Rick said. "We heard you're now an executive."

"Yeah," Steve smiled. "Surprised the hell out of me! I literally slept my way to the top. From porn star to executive in a few short months."

"So you'll be taking charge of the studio?"

"Yeah. Gabriel's moved on to bigger things, and the company liked what they saw in my resume. With Gabe's backing, there really wasn't any doubt I would get the position."

"It's better money," Sandy said, "and he isn't doing any more sex scenes." Amy cooed in her arms.

"But he was so good!" James groaned playfully.

"Don't I know it!" she exclaimed. "But I'm happy to have him to myself again. Plus, we always have the awards to remind us. Don't we, sweetie?"

"That's right!" Steve puffed up with faux pride. "Best Anal Scene by a New-comer, right here, gentlemen!"

"Poor Ruth," Terrence reflected dramatically, secretly wishing he had a swelling musical score backing him a la Greer Garson. "Dying on her 81st birthday. But she had a good life, I suppose."

"Well, at least she died happy," David offered. "Being given a lap dance by one of the go-go boys from *Vera's*."

"I'm just glad it wasn't me giving her that dance," Cliff said. "I don't think I would have gotten over it. She was a sweet old lady."

"So why did she end up giving the house to you?" David inquired of Terrence.

Terrence shrugged. "I don't know exactly why she chose me specifically. You know she always said she was going to give it to one of the Boys. I guess she figured you and Cliff already had a place, so I was next in line."

"Well, it didn't take you long to refurnish the place," David said.

"That was the fun part," Christian offered. "Dad and I have been antique shopping every weekend. We've found some great stuff!"

"Moving in for good, are you?" Cliff smiled.

"Yep," Christian nodded. "I'm a permanent resident now. Mom was really cool about it."

"Well, she's had you long enough. I get you until college," Terrence said. "Even though that's only a year away."

"You're doing some shopping and remodeling of your own," Christian noted to David and Cliff.

"Yeah, we're expanding the living room, tearing down the wall between it and the guest room. We finally have enough money to put in a pool." David held tight to his new husband.

"Bitch!" Terrence griped. "Right as I move out! You did that on purpose!"

"What? Living practically rent-free wasn't good enough for you?" David kidded. "Besides, I didn't have that kind of money until now. With me being the editor of *Gay Men's Fitness* and Cliff competing full-time in bodybuilding, we're making a decent living."

"Ah, yes," Terrence sighed. "In one year, the porn industry loses both you and Steve. How will it ever recover?"

"Oh, I think there are plenty of new up-and-coming stars to keep it going," Cliff said with a shrewd grin. He nodded their attention in the direction of the bar. Becky Ridgeworth was walking toward it with a handsomely built young man. "You'll be hearing about that one."

Melinda stood quietly by the bar, still nervous, but hopeful. Hope was a marvelous thing.

It was nice to see Patrick having such a good time with his girlfriend and with those around him. The neighborhood loved him. He had become one of the Boys. It was sweet how he and Rachel had spent time with her while she stood alone and friendless. His smile made everything seem better. Was this what being a good mother felt like? The guilt and pain of losing him had forged in her a stronger love, which had only increased at the realization of how resilient he really was. Her previous ignorance had almost destroyed their entire relationship, not to mention his future, but he had bounced back and actually forgiven her for it.

She took a quick drink from her glass of punch. She grimaced faintly. It was spiked. She could taste the rum. In the old days, she would have complained and made a scene. But now ... Well, she rather liked the dangerous taste on her tongue. It was new and different, which was just what she needed. This was another addition to an endless line of new experiences.

Nanna wouldn't approve. She smiled at the thought. *Who cares?* She knocked back the rest of the punch in one swig at the thought. Nanna was in a seniors' center off in the Bible Belt ... And, godammit, they could keep her! Even conversing with her in short spurts on the phone was too much.

"Mel," Becky called, walking toward her. She was arm-in-arm with a very handsome young man.

Melinda and Becky had become sociable. They weren't friends, but they were at least sociable.

"This is my date, Trent," Becky introduced the young man. He smiled at Melinda with perfect white teeth. His black hair was swept back like some Hollywood matinee idol of old.

"Hi," he said awkwardly, like a nervous boy at a school dance.

"He's been wanting to meet you, but was too shy. I work with him," Becky explained.

"Hello, Trent," Melinda greeted, holding out her hand. He took it and kissed it gently. "You wanted to meet me? Whatever for?"

"I'll leave you two alone," Becky said, scurrying off before Melinda could object.

The two of them stood anxious and quiet.

"Are you and Becky a couple?" she inquired as a form of pleasantry.

"No, not at all," he replied. "We work at the studio together, that's all."

"Oh," she said. "Well, you must work with a lot of pretty women there."

"Yeah, but none of them are really my type. Finding the right lady for me has been a slow and disappointing process."

She liked his voice. He seemed courteous. Exactly the type of guy she would have dated if she had been allowed to date when she was younger. Too bad she wasn't closer to his age.

"You are, though," he offered, with a hint of fear in his voice.

"Me?"

"You want to dance? Please don't say no. I couldn't stand being turned down by the prettiest lady here."

She stood for a moment, calming the fears and negative voices in her head. He wanted to dance? Why would he want to dance with her? He was so handsome!

She didn't know what it was that made her inhibitions suddenly fly away-the alcohol, the night air, the music-but she placed her empty glass on the bar, swallowed hard, and gave Trent her hand.

"I would love to," she said.

978-0-595-45482-2
0-595-45482-8

Made in the USA
Middletown, DE
18 August 2016